To Lesu...

from

Anita

# The
# Mid-Life
# Ex-Wife

A novel

A. M. Hodge

Eloquent Books
New York, New York

Eloquent Books
An imprint of AEG Publishing Group
845 Third Avenue, 6th Floor—6016
New York, NY 10022
http://www.eloquentbooks.com


ISBN: 978-1-60693-644-3, 1-60693-644-1


Book Designer: Bruce Salender


Printed in the United States of America

*This above all: to thine own self be true,*
*And it must follow, as the night the day,*
*Thou canst not then be false to any man.*

—Shakespeare: *Hamlet,* Act 1

# Disclaimer

This is a novel, one of a multitude of plausible stories about how an imaginary couple might have experienced the process of a mid-life divorce. The characters and non-specific locations are fictitious, and are not intended to resemble real places, or persons either living or dead. Opinions expressed by the characters do not necessarily reflect those of the author.

# Dedication

This novel is dedicated to all mid-life ex-wives—may you find happiness, and prosper.

# PART 1

# In the Beginning

Early that morning, as the dawn of a new day bathed everything in a rosy glow, Alice turned over in bed and entered a brief mythical dream. This same dream had already visited her twice this week. In it, Alice walked along a path covered by layers of leaves, meandering through a grove of trees that were no more than meager sticks. It was a landscape of poverty, exposed in thin gray light. From a branch, the bird that chattered at her resembled a roughly chiseled and painted wood carving that had come to life. It called, "Now or never, now or never, now or never..."

Alice pushed the blanket aside, as she awakened to the twitter of nesting house finches in the English ivy outside the window. A seagull mewed in the distance. Her husband Ralph lay in the bed with her, an isolated figure concealed in a swaddle of sheets and blankets, lightly snoring in a dream of his own. A wisp of hair at the edge of the bald spot beginning to spread on the crown of his head—the only part of his body that lay revealed—rose and fell with each breath.

Regarding the mummy that was Ralph, Alice remembered her feelings, when as a young mother she fell deeply in love for the first time with a man who was not her husband. The shock of it brought on the demise of the sweet, youthful, dead-end exclusivity of that stage of their marriage. The experience propelled her headlong into a more complex emotional world. She became willful, and determined to have a love affair. For a few minutes she lay there, recollecting what was an important relationship for her although it had not become sexual. Later, when she met Brad, she experienced another fundamental change. He became first a friend, then a lover. The ache that accompanied her memory of him had subsided over the years but it still remained alive deep within her heart. She concluded from her experiences with men, that you attract what you are, and you respond according to your own vulnerabilities.

As she looked at Ralph, she recalled how strongly she had felt the need to wall off her marriage before she could get involved with another man. Only the object of her desire was important, no one else, especially not her husband. It wasn't fair but it did express some ancient visceral need to isolate an affair from marriage and family.

When Ralph learned about Brad, he reacted to the truth that her affections had wandered away from him, so much so that he knelt in the middle of their bed pounding the mattress shouting, "Why? Why? Why? Don't…you…love…me…?"

She remembered how thoroughly his behavior had immobilized her. She wondered if she gave that same performance for him right now, what Ralph would do. Would it unwrap the mummy? Would he remember that earlier occasion? Might he laugh and ask her if she had lost it?

Each trespass drives a wedge between the partners of a marriage. Each repetition widens the gap. The wider the gap becomes, the less likely the partners will be able to bridge it and reconnect with each other; that is, if they want to return, or if they believe they could. Alice knew there was not even the remotest chance for that kind of effort to now be worth considering; it could not possibly succeed.

Alice had even consulted a psychologist. She tried to be very contained in talking about her relationship with Ralph. Only after she spent some minutes describing their day to day life did she notice the man's attention concentrated on her hands. She had folded them in her lap when she sat down. Now they had come to life without her permission. Her own body was very effectively preempting Alice's awkward effort to communicate. Horrified, she became aware of her right forefinger jabbing through the loop made by her left thumb and forefinger. She forced her hands to stop, a silent embarrassed tear streaking down her cheek.

The psychologist gently reached out to her, patted her arm and made a suggestion. "You said that you have a boat and sometimes spend a weekend on it. Isn't that a romantic setting? Can't you sail someplace to get away and relax? Out on the water, by yourselves, you'd be in a place where you could seduce him. You're an attractive woman. He'd certainly respond." It had seemed reasonable enough, and with another man it might have worked, but by then Alice was well beyond the point of mustering sufficient strength to make even a feeble assault on the fortress. At Ralph's insistence, they still shared a bed. That was the extent of the pretence that there was anything left between them. She understood the energy and determination needed to construct and maintain such a walled-off presence. If there's no longer any connection why not at least admit that, and accommodate to it? She left him in peace.

In the course of their life together—right up to this moment—when Ralph asserted and pronounced, Alice deferred and retreated. Even when Alice first admitted there must be a separation—in spite of her promise to Ralph that she would try her best to pull their marriage back together—that did not become her immediate focus. Each time she traveled to the brink, she backed away. She firmly reminded herself that by the end of this day her life would have turned in a different direction. She got up, went to the kitchen, started the coffee, and then sat staring out the window onto the quiet harbor.

Two days ago she filed for a divorce. This morning she had to find a way to tell him. She wondered what to do and to say, how to do it all with the least amount of hurt. Too many years of a marriage that had long since died were coming to an end, and as that strange wooden bird called out in her dream, it *was* now or never.

    Alice knew that this might well be the last opportunity she would ever have for making such a drastic move to completely change the course of her life. It had taken her years to recover from losing Brad. During that ordeal of personal grieving, she had worked hard for their daughter's sake to mend her marriage with Ralph. She had learned to be honest with and to respect herself. Now she had mustered the courage to act.

# Alice

From the start of their relationship, Ralph found Alice both admirable and formidable. Unlike him, she had grown up with immigrant children as her schoolmates. Powerfully motivated by their parents, these friends were very competitive. They were driven by the idea that only education could change their lives by ensuring financial success. Alice absorbed their credo—the more one learned the better. In her mind, education became the only answer to how she could transform her life. When Alice completed high school, she was prepared to go on to college. Her mother encouraged her to find work as a book-keeper, but like her friends, Alice wanted nothing less than to become an astronaut. It was a struggle, but with a scholarship and savings from the meager salary she earned from part time jobs, Alice began college.

She met Ralph in her junior year. They began dating and when they broke up, Alice became more involved with the group of students that constituted her circle of friends. There was one, Eric, of whom Alice was especially fond. She saw him on a daily basis; they shared some classes and over time, developed a close friendship. They sat in the library or cafeteria together for hours, talking and working on homework assignments, sometimes joined by other students. In time, Alice began to think of Eric and herself as a possible couple. He never broached the topic to her, nor she to him. Then she bumped into Ralph at a party, and they began to date once more. Things soon became serious between them. Ralph was nearing graduation, but Alice still had a year remaining before she would get her degree. Both expected to finish college, get a job and begin a career. Then they could think about settling down. As time went on, and their relationship deepened, both assumed that would mean marriage.

One weekend, Alice accepted Ralph's invitation to drive to New Hampshire for the day. It was beautiful early fall weather. The sky was clear blue, and the sun pleasantly warm. They stopped for lunch, and then hiked to the top of Mount Monadnock from which they could clearly see the Boston skyline. Descending, they returned to the car and drove just a short distance before Ralph turned in to a grove of evergreens and parked. They stepped out of the car to stretch their legs. Ralph reached for her breasts, kissing her as she struggled against him. His hands traveled urgently down the sides of her body, pulling her clothing along with them. He pinned her down onto a bed of pine needles, slid her pants down and penetrated her. It was soon finished. He gave her a quick kiss and helped her onto her feet.

On the drive home, he was ebullient. She was distressed, physically and emotionally. Was this how men claimed ownership of a woman's affections? He treated her like a conquest; she was a human being, worthy of kindness and respect. Unlike all those novels she had read, Alice did not emerge from this encounter as a kind of defiant, smoldering heroine of fiction. She was afraid of his behavior toward her, and worried about whether there would be consequences.

A few weeks later, she told him she thought she might be pregnant. Once that was verified, they talked about what they would do. It seemed best for them to marry. They probably would have anyway. Her career would be deferred for a time. The wedding and reception were equally attended by Ralph's family and their friends, and Alice's family and her friends.

Her wedding dress was loaned by a cousin, as there seemed little sense in buying her own. On that day, she was a radiant bride looking forward to the future. Both families seemed satisfied with their union.

# Ralph

I met Alice when I was finishing college and she was just a sophomore. I thought she was good-looking, but she was not from my part of town. By that I mean to date her, I had a long drive across the city to get to her house. In those days I owned a '58 Chevy which all the guys envied. I loved that car. I could go to the White Mountains every weekend, stay with my friends up there, have a great time and then easily make it back for my first class on Monday morning.

That got me out of the house for the weekend. It was tough living at home. Dad was a second-generation Irishman who worked hard to support the family. He worked since he was just a boy, doing odd jobs and carrying newspapers door to door in the neighborhood. Now he was a business executive and we lived in a colonial style house filled with expensive antiques. He loved that house. He bought it just after he married my mother. He hated the thought of doing it, but he borrowed the money from her uncle. Dad worked hard to pay it back as soon as he could. He was proud of that.

After a busy day at the office, he'd let off steam by stopping for drinks with the guys on the way home from work, then had a couple more when he got home. By the time dinner was over, Dad was ready for an evening of well-lubricated discussion that could cover a lot of territory, but what he loved best was politics. I thought it was interesting and fun when my parents invited friends over for dinner, especially those who loved to throw it right back at him. Some of those sessions turned into real mayhem, but however hot and loud they got, everyone enjoyed it. Nights that we had no company were sometimes difficult. Dad would sit in front of the TV with a drink in his hand and talk back to the newscasters. Once in a while he even made a good point. Sometimes he'd just yell at them if he didn't like what they were saying. He rarely interrupted Walter Cronkite, so my mother and I figured Dad really respected him.

Not long after I brought Alice home to meet my folks, Dad must have decided that she was a worthy opponent. Maybe in his own way he just wanted to put her in her place. Alice was interested in conservation. Dad loved to rant about "do-gooders" who were out to save the world. For whatever reason, Dad really looked forward to opportunities to duke it out with her. The signs of serious confrontation were Dad's stentorian voice expanding to fill the room, and Alice's voice lowering an octave and turning plummy. Mom and I would sit in front of the TV, pretending there was something more interesting on the tube. Nothing could beat the entertainment value of Dad going at it with Alice. She gave it back pretty well, and if it looked like she was just a point or two away from carrying the argument, he'd switch gears and start on something else. She was always angry when he did this, which probably made him happy.

\*\*\*

Some of the guys I hung out with thought Alice was a hot number, but a real "ice queen" socially. So we made a bet as to who would get to her first. Being better looking than the others, I thought I'd have the advantage. I was right.

On the weekends, for a while I mostly went off with the guys, but then that got a bit dull and I stopped going so often. Alice and I kept dating; we were together a lot. In her last year at college, after a weekend in the mountains together, we became a couple. I made sure that everybody knew it, too—that I had scored with Alice. Then she told me she was pregnant. When we went to talk with the priest about a wedding, he said it was long past the time when we probably would have been married, if we both hadn't been in school. That kind of relieved some of the guilt we both felt.

My parents were beside themselves when I told them we had to get married. First they wanted to make me tell Alice I didn't believe it was my kid, but I couldn't do that. I knew I was the father. I had bragged about it to the guys, so I could hardly change my mind about that. Mom and Dad finally agreed to put the best face on it, and come to the wedding. My sister Penelope thought it was funny.

My mother asked Alice if it was all right for her to wear her favorite black dress to the wedding. I nearly passed out when I heard her say that. Alice was incredibly nervous about the whole thing and told her, "Fine if that's what you want." She even sounded friendly when she said it, like it really didn't matter one way or the other.

It was a small wedding. I refused to wear a wedding ring, just to get the message across to Alice that she may have married me, but still, I felt cheated by the circumstances. I was so embarrassed and disgusted with her and with myself that I told her on our wedding night I wasn't going to touch her then or maybe ever again. Well, that was silly of me because I just couldn't help myself in that department, not then anyway. Besides, what else could happen? She was already pregnant and now she was my wife.

It wasn't until later that Alice told her folks the baby was coming sooner than she had said. I thought they would hate me for it, but would have to forgive me because after all, I did marry her. They were thrilled when Melanie was born and they became grandparents for the first time. Later, Alice's father said that it was probably the only way she would ever have gotten married and had children. They had decided that she would always be a career woman and would probably never settle down to have a family. They were all totally out of their minds when Melanie arrived. She was a beautiful baby, the perfect blond angel. She looked like my side of the family. She was gorgeous. As it turned out, she was to be our only child.

# Alice

When Melanie was a few years old, Alice ventured out of her home to seek volunteer conservation work. Ralph worried about them growing apart. After a couple of years of volunteering, Alice wanted to move on to something that would provide a steady paycheck. Ralph had begun to complain about the household bills. He would spread them out on the kitchen table and leave them for days at a time, seemingly on display. When she asked what he thought he was doing, he became evasive, saying his family might care to know how much he provided for their support.

One day, Melanie came home sick from school. Her teacher, Mrs. Merryfield, sent a note with her asking both parents to come for a conference the next evening. She explained to them that Melanie was anxious about the family being in debt. It seemed the child had added up the amounts of the bills and could not imagine that much money. The teacher asked point blank, "Have you lost your job? I can't imagine another reason why Melanie has taken on such outsized worries. It isn't right for a child to think she has to help solve the problem of the family debts."

Mrs. Merryfield was very concerned about the little girl, and grew increasingly indignant on her behalf when Ralph laughed and explained that his father always did that so everyone could appreciate the cost of running a household.

"But still," the teacher insisted, "it is not appropriate for such a young child to be burdened like that. Maybe an older child can understand it, but a younger one certainly cannot. Your Melanie's become ill and she cannot concentrate on her school work. It is not fair to her."

After that experience, Alice felt it more incumbent on her than ever to find a paying job, and she stepped up her effort. Ralph did not want her to go to work. Men of his father's generation openly expressed their belief that when a wife went to work it was because the husband was not doing his duty to earn enough money to support his family. If a woman even worked at all it was usually temporary, while she looked for a husband.

Did Ralph, deep down, really subscribe to that anachronistic way of seeing things? Both his mother and aunt were college graduates. His aunt worked all her life as a nurse. His mother had not. It was a point of pride for Ralph's father that his wife was a homemaker and never had to work outside the house. Alice grew up understanding these were the ground rules for some people, but she was not willing to be bound by them. Both of her parents worked, and Alice wanted to work to accomplish things in her own life. By the sacrifices she made to attend college, she had long ago served ample notice of her aspirations. In fact, that was where she met Ralph. She harbored no secrets about her desire to live what she imagined to be a full and productive life.

The initial battle that Ralph waged against Alice came as she began her first job after their marriage. It emerged from the very depths of his manhood. By then, Alice had been a housewife and mother for long enough that Melanie was already in school. That first job was a symbolic step forward into the next phase of her life, although at the time, neither she nor Ralph would have identified it as such. His reaction to her new role was as primitive as it was brutal. Ralph rebelled, not openly, but in his own way. On the nights before Alice had to be up early to get herself and their daughter out the door to meet the school bus, that is, five consecutive nights a week, Alice dropped into bed exhausted as soon as Melanie finished her homework and was tucked in for the night. She would fall immediately into a deep dreamless sleep. About an hour later, Ralph would ascend the stairs to their bedroom, then wake her, force himself on her, and return to the living room to watch TV. At midnight, when he would be ready to retire for the night, he once again woke her and repeated his performance. Pounding him on the chest and yelling in his face had no effect on him. By now, Alice would be so angry that she could not sleep. By about 3 a.m., if she were lucky, a light fitful doze might overtake her. At 4 a.m., he would roll over on her and without even seeming to wake up, Ralph would take her yet again. Alice would cry until 5 a.m. when the alarm went off. Ralph never remembered the next day what he had done to her during the previous night. Whether he could not remember, or did not care to admit to it, he consistently and vehemently denied his behavior.

If she were able to take Melanie and leave, she would have. But then what would she do? Even though she worked, she didn't earn enough income to support herself and her daughter. She had no other place to go, so she stuck it out for as long as it lasted. Ralph went on exercising his unconscious insistent "conjugal rights" until Alice collapsed and could not return to work for a while. Her crisis happened on a night when Ralph was taking a client out to dinner.

One of Alice's friends recently died of cancer. Thea had small children, and on the night she died, she locked herself in the bathroom. When her husband found the location of her body, he had to break down the door to get to her. It seemed no one could believe what Thea had done. Some expressed the opinion that she had been stupid to do that. No one seemed equipped to understand it. That night Alice learned exactly why Thea locked that door. It was obvious to anyone who was a mother. Thea loved her babies very dearly and did not want them to be the first to discover her body.

On the night of Alice's breakdown, she was home with

Melanie. Just after she put her daughter to bed, tightness seized her chest. She had never experienced that kind of pain before and it frightened her. Automatically she went upstairs to the bathroom and locked the door. She lay on the floor as waves of dizziness and nausea swept over her. She cried her sorrow and frustration to the empty room. After a while, the episode passed. She continued to lay there and was soon soaked in sweat. Then she got up, went to bed, wrapping herself tightly in the blankets to warm and comfort her chilled body. When Ralph finally came home and found her in bed, she told him what had happened. She said she thought she was having a heart attack, and was so scared that she called the family doctor. She would see him the very next morning unless something else happened during the night. Ralph never repeated his marathon sexual performances with her after that.

Alice never told a soul about this until she was meeting with her divorce counselor, and then only after she came to feel comfortable with Carrie. She learned that this experience was no rare phenomenon. Carrie made her understand that Ralph's behavior was no fault of Alice's, and set some of those demons to rest. But all that came much later in her life.

# Ralph

I loved my wife and my daughter, and life was good. My single friends teased me but I didn't care. What I had then was worth a whole lot more than all the talk about one-night-stands, bragging rights and who was scoring with whom. None of that kid stuff was important to me any more.

We moved from our city apartment and bought a house way out in the country. We lived in a pretty remote place and it wasn't long before Alice was unhappy at not being able to do some of the things she had when she lived in the city. She learned to drive so that once we got a second car, I didn't have to come home from work in the middle of the day to take her and Melanie to the doctor, or impose on a neighbor when we needed that kind of help. That little bit of independence for Alice freed me to do my job without worrying about what was going on at home. I could also do what I wanted after work. Mostly that was stopping for a drink with the guys. I never called Alice when I did that because I thought I didn't have to report in. My father never called my mother when he decided to stop for a drink after work with his buddies. He probably thought it'd look like Mom was in control of him. Alice didn't have me tied to her apron strings either. When I would get home late, she would always be furious with me for staying out and for not telling her where I was. I always felt more powerful over her when that happened. There was something I could do that she couldn't control, not that she ever thought much about that with Melanie to keep her busy.

***

My job changed, so we started looking for a house nearer my new office. With Melanie growing up and almost ready to start school, Alice wanted to be in a town with a good school system. We found an antique that we loved at first sight. My parents objected to the house and even though they hardly ever talked to each other, called Alice's parents to try to get them to weigh in as well, to so-called "bring us to our senses." We were in love, and excited about living in a historic house, so we bought the place in spite of what our parents thought. It had been featured in a home and garden magazine some time in the early '30's, and the pile of old photos from that convinced my father that this might be okay after all. That provided some kind of pedigree for the place in his mind. My mother always went along with him, and usually gave in to whatever he wanted. Once he decided the old house was okay with him, it was fine with her as well.

You could almost feel the way life had been lived there over the past centuries. The rooms were small and the ceilings were low. Nothing in that old house was straight or level. I had to bend down to go through any doorway. I guess there were no tall people in the family that originally built the place. It was a great house for Melanie, with all its nooks and crannies and hiding places. Because we were outside of the main part of the town, we had some land and there was some undeveloped acreage adjacent to us. That provided plenty of room for all the animals Alice and Melanie brought home.

Alice was a hard worker—both her parents worked—so she was never comfortable with the idea of staying at home like my mother did. She really found herself when she volunteered for conservation work. She saw an ad in the local paper, called the number and said she would like to help them out. For a while she was happy just to have something outside the house to do. She always acted like she was on a mission with that stuff.

Her nights out at conservation meetings gave me more chances to stop off with the guys on the way home. I kind of slipped into a pattern of doing that a couple of times a week. Of course, I would never call her to say what I was doing. Then there was the night they kept on going and I went right along with them. I was the only one who had never worn a wedding ring. The others took theirs off and slipped them into their pockets. A couple of the guys actually had tan lines that showed where the rings had been. We picked up some girls and when it was all over, it was already morning. Uh-oh, this was going to mean trouble. I went home. Alice was already up of course, helping Melanie get ready to meet the school bus. Melanie looked at me like she knew what I had been doing, out all night. It was not the kind of a look you expect to get from a little kid. Then Alice gave me a look that went right through me. "Damn," she said. "I just decided how I was going to spend the insurance money."

Then she turned her back on me. That was hard. I sure got that message—she wanted me DOA if I was ever again gone all night. It would be the only excuse acceptable to her. After that I made sure to call her if I was going to be late.

*** 

A couple of weeks later, I thought I really had her for a change. One day I came home early from work. Melanie and some of her friends were running around in the yard, along with the mob of cats and dogs that always seemed to show up when the kids were playing outside. There was a strange pickup truck parked in front of the house right on the street. I asked the kids whose truck that was. A chorus of voices answered, "It belongs to Hank. He's upstairs in the bedroom with Mommy."

Well, that's all I needed. She wasn't expecting me home this early so she was upstairs entertaining a boyfriend. If I had stopped to think about it, I would have known that was way too obvious to be true. She wouldn't do that, especially not with all these kids running in and out of the house. But I didn't stop to think. I was much too excited. Adrenalin surged through my body and I swung into action.

I thought, "This is too good to be true." I was elated at the idea that now I had her by the short hairs. She was not going to get off easily. "This is shameful," I thought, imagining the scene playing out before a sympathetic judge and jury. "She's up in our bedroom with some guy in the middle of the afternoon with all these kids running around outside unsupervised. Some excuse for a mother she is." I smirked, "Boy oh boy! I've got that sanctimonious bitch right where I want her. She'll never ever again make trouble for me about staying out late and not calling her to let her know where I am. I've got her now."

My feet pounded on the cement floor as I ran through the garage and headed into the house. I ran slowly so I could make more noise. I kept going, stomping my feet as if I were wearing hobnail boots, pounding the old floors in the rooms downstairs until the original half-trees that supported them were shaking. I was so convinced of my expected triumph over Alice, that each time I slammed my foot down, I did it with even more weight and purpose.

I hesitated when I came to the short staircase that led straight up into the bedroom. They knew I was there, so no reason to rush. And then, with extra emphasis, I pounded my way up each one of the nine steep steps. All the doorways in the house were too short for me, but this one was even shorter, so I had to bow my way into the bedroom. Once inside, I raised my head, straightened up to my full height and looked straight ahead, directly at the bed. It was undisturbed. In the middle of the room Alice and a man she knew from the Town, both fully clothed, stood talking. They turned toward me just as I made my entrance through that low doorway.

It was apparent they were talking about the house and how it had been restored back in the '20's and '30's. Alice liked to show the house to anyone who appreciated antiques. One of the stops on her usual tour was in the upstairs bedroom and small dressing room on the opposite side of the massive central chimney where some "King's boards" had been used in the walls. There were also a number of small places that Alice recently discovered where the restorer had patched the paneling, so closely matching the pieces with the original boards that his work was nearly invisible. Alice loved to show this stuff off, especially to anyone who understood their significance without her having to go into great detail to explain it.

Of course, all the kids came running right behind me like a tribe of wild animals. They flowed in through the small doorway, surrounding the adults, and filling the room to witness this grown-up encounter. The small visitors were sure to carry home their various tales of what they'd seen at our house. Word would spread. It would make a very juicy story.

Alice gave me a cold hard look. I saw Hank catch her expression and barely contain an amused grin. Trying to put the best face on things, Alice attempted to act as if I just made my normal entry. She pretended the noise and stomping were for the benefit of the kids, who loved dumb adult performances. "Ralph, you remember Hank. He and his wife have a house a lot like ours and nearly the same age over on Acorn Street, about two miles from here."

I just stood there feeling like a fool. Alice was giving her usual house tour to someone who really *was* interested in seeing things like where and how restorations had been done that fooled the casual eye, someone who *might* actually be impressed by the "King's boards." Yes, I remembered Hank. He was a pretty well respected guy in the Town. I had heard his name before, and knew who he was. And now Hank knew who I was. So what could I do but join in the conversation and pretend that I always acted like an idiot when I came home early—always came into the house that very same way just to let everyone know I was home. I knew that any future time that I might run into Hank, it would remind me of this. But I also knew that guys are guys and would always stick together. Hank would never let on if he even bothered to remember this encounter.

# Alice

When Alice returned to school to complete a second college degree, Ralph admitted that he was afraid of losing her to some other man she might meet and find more interesting. He was uneasy about her spending more time with other people, away from home. He was nervous and acted like he was deeply distressed that things could change between them. Alice did her best to reassure him. Her need sprang from the volunteer conservation work which had struck a chord that resonated deep within her. She sought a more profound understanding of how the natural world functioned and now had her sights set on learning about ecology. She still believed in the power of education to make life happier and more successful. Alice was shocked that Ralph could even imagine that she would leave him. After all, they were a team, and were raising a daughter. They had married in the Church. Wasn't that supposed to last forever? Weren't people supposed to grow and change as they went through life? Wasn't this just that kind of opportunity? Why couldn't he understand? He finally relented in the face of her determination.

Alice became a biologist. It provided a context for her life that gave her a powerful understanding and appreciation for her fellow creatures, human and animal. She developed a profound sense of belonging in the world. There was an ease in knowing there was a niche for her in the natural scheme of things. She felt grounded in an unblemished kind of peace, one that grew naturally from her identity, not as something special but as a part of a global community of all living things. Alice walked the woods with her dog, paralleling the streams that ran near their seventeenth century home. She observed the birds, and noted evidence of animals like beaver and muskrat. She followed secret brambled paths that led past old farm fences and stone foundations, and trod an old cart path that evoked past lives industriously spent. She went out some evenings, and on one foggy night, slowly approaching her like four huge apparitions in the mist, Alice met four horses walking slowly past, on a quest of their own to seek out a neighbor's vegetable garden. She felt the warmth of the earth expiring into the cool air of moonlit October evenings, smelled wood smoke from her own and neighbors' hearths. Contentment filled her soul.

\*\*\*

When did Alice first learn that her heart could close to Ralph? Was it the first time she knew he had been unfaithful to her? When that happened, the common attitude about such things was "boys will be boys." Women of her generation would be expected to take it in stride: cry a little, whether copious tears or genteel sobbing. Banish him from the bedroom for a couple of nights—if you must. Exact just the right amount of contrition before you re-admit him. Accept offerings of the customary penances of flowers or chocolates, if he thinks to make any. Get on with your life. Choose your confidants carefully. You never know who may have a selfish interest in learning that your husband has a wandering eye.

Perhaps it was the first time she felt herself attracted to another man. Alice was young and unprepared when it first happened. She berated herself for disloyalty. Then she had to acknowledge that man was one she might have married if they had met under other circumstances and in the earlier years of their lives. That was an intense, unexpected, and not altogether welcome surprise.

There was a different experience when Alice returned to college to study biology. Alice met Bruce when she went to the college to find out about enrolling as an older student. He had been courtly and respectful of her desire to continue her education. Bruce was enchanted by her and strongly encouraged her to return to school. "More and more people are returning as adults to make changes and adjustments to their careers and to increase the quality of their lives. If you like, I'll be glad to serve as your academic advisor. I'm doing a paper for the college's administration about this new phenomenon of older students returning into our system. You're a prime example of what I think is going to become an important trend in education."

Flattered, she agreed, and Bruce became a part of her life. At first he acted strictly as her advisor. In time, she sought him out as a friend. He began to seek her out for a love affair. Alice couldn't do that. Not with him. Her marriage to Ralph remained intact.

***

When did Ralph's heart first close to Alice? Was it the first time he went out with the boys and stayed out all night, never calling to let her know he was all right, or where he was? That experience reinforced his feeling of power over her. He could do anything he wanted and she had to deal with it. After all, he married her when she got pregnant with his kid. She owed him.

Was it on another occasion that this happened, when Ralph fled from Alice's presence to avoid a confrontation about an affair? Was that the time, when he was angry, afraid and unwilling to apologize?

Was it later when they both attended a therapy session where Ralph's counselor confronted Alice with a shouting accusation about being stuck in the past and not getting over it? The woman had stood before Alice bellowing in her face, "Oh, so now you want to talk about some stupid thing that happened five years ago? You want to relive the past? Who needs that?

What about now? What's the matter with you anyway, keeping grudges like that? No wonder we can never get anywhere!"

Alice's face crumpled in pained hopelessness. She became totally silent and did not even try to respond to anything the counselor shouted at her. Alice's burning issue was that she could never get closure with Ralph on anything. She could not pin him down. They couldn't talk about anything so nothing could ever be settled. Each unresolved issue fed into the next. Her wounds had thus remained open and festering. Alice needed healing. That wasn't going to happen there.

None of the joint efforts worked. By the time they were both willing to admit there was need for intervention of some kind, there was too much anger, too much past history not addressed and still painfully thriving between them. Separate counseling did have some benefits, although those were dubious. Each had someone who focused on their individual needs. They could talk about their sessions with each other afterward—if they chose—editing out the things they weren't prepared to share.

Ralph's point of view prevailed over any attempt to initiate mutual discussion to seek understanding. Agreement was not the anticipated goal. Simply expressed, it amounted to "You fix it while I go away. Let me know when it's safe to come back." Any such effort would always be one-sided. Alice could not afford that kind of vulnerability. Neither therefore practiced confessing their sins, or the secrets of their hearts to anyone— and most especially not to each other. Alice experienced Ralph's emotional absence as a physical feeling of a cold wind blowing at her back. He had opened a door into a different life, and awarded himself free passage through it whenever it suited him. She was left behind in the old life, exposed and at risk. For a long time, she either didn't realize it, or could not admit it to herself.

Each new hint that something was amiss placed Alice in a different vantage point with a slightly different perspective on things. She felt like a human kaleidoscope, the same shards of glittering glass falling to form different patterns as the instrument rotated. Which of these shifting patterns were truths, which deceptions? Which were real, which were misleading? She could never be quite certain.

# Ralph

Against my wishes, Alice went to work. She saved enough money to buy a small boat. She went sailing in it with her friends, once or twice a week, depending on the tides. It didn't interest me at first. Then one day she asked me if I wanted to go sailing with her. When we were out in the bay, Alice handed me the mainsheet and the tiller. I was hooked at the moment I felt the wind and the water bite, with me holding the boat on course by controlling the mainsail and the rudder. I felt very differently about boats from that moment on. If I could be in control like that, then I wanted to sail with Alice anywhere she wanted to go.

During the first years we sailed together a lot, with Melanie and sometimes one of the dogs. We had great fun. The boats got bigger as our daughter grew up and we began to cruise, each year ranging farther from home. Finally, we sailed all the way to Maine, the best place we had ever been. We returned year after year, experiencing new places each time, as well as anchorages we had visited on other cruises. Those were happy years. Alice worked right along with me, especially in the boatyard in the spring getting ready to launch, and in the fall after the boat was pulled for the winter. We were a team. I was in charge. That felt great. I wanted it to last just like that for the rest of our lives.

# Alice

Ralph came into his own as a sailor as he discovered his passion for the sea. In the beginning, the family traveled together. The boats increased in size as the years progressed. The family began traveling longer distances on their summer cruises, and had to pack more gear aboard for extended time spent on the water. Finally, Ralph began a charter business to justify the expense of keeping a large boat. Each year they brought the vessel north to a yard in Maine that handled the business end of their summer charters. They vacationed at the end of the season and in the fall, returned the yacht to their home port for winter storage.

On one trip north, a two-day venture, the family spent the night in a cove at the mouth of the Annisquam River on Cape Ann. Before first light, they dropped the mooring and started out into the Gulf of Maine. The weather forecast predicted a cloudy and windy day with strong gusts developing as the day progressed. They motored with the mainsail set to steady the boat's motion, and went along nicely while sheltered by the receding Cape. They approached the Isles of Shoals, and noted Appledore, Smutty Nose, and other of the Isles as they passed. Downwind and still in the lee of the islands, breezes wafted the fragrance of their fields over the water toward the receding craft. Alice enjoyed the meadowy perfume for as long as it lasted, and kept warm the memory of those moments for years afterward.

A blast of wind and choppy seas buffeting the sails and hull signaled they were outside of the land's protection and now in open waters. Under leaden skies, the rocky desolation of Boon Island was quickly left astern. The next sign of a welcoming shore would not be sighted until they were closer to Portland and its beaming lighthouse. They sailed most of the day this way, experiencing a combination of choppy seas that changed to quartering swells as the tide turned.

Alice succumbed to seasickness shortly after she spent time below in the galley preparing a hot lunch for everyone. Melanie lasted a while longer, tuned in to her CD's via a set of headphones. Then it was up to Ralph to maintain the boat's course. As the wind increased, they decided to pull in to Casco Bay and shelter in a cove in one of the outer islands. As the boat passed by an evocatively named rock, "Junk of Pork," Melanie leaned out over the leeward side and succumbed to the imagined smell of cold greasy meat. With little help from the others, Ralph steered the vessel into the small cove where he dropped and set the anchor for the night.

Seasickness is a terrible thing to have to endure. Miraculously, it vanishes almost at once when the pitching and yawing motions subside, allowing the vessel to steady and it becomes possible to move about without having to constantly balance against a lurching hull.

"We'll finish the run up the Sheepscot tomorrow," said Ralph, visibly agitated at the idea of being a day late to arrive at the boatyard. He made a call to the charter agent on the ship-to-shore radio, and then left it on to hear other boats in the area talking about weather conditions along the coast. As they tidied the deck and settled in, another vessel made its entrance into the cove. Alice was positive she saw an Atlantic sturgeon off Boon Island, and was just then sharing that information as she and Ralph settled down in the cockpit with steaming cups of coffee. Ralph noted and then hailed the approaching craft.

Once they were safely anchored, Ralph got into the dinghy and rowed over to talk with them.

They were an older couple who had set out from Boston that morning. Off Boon Island, they told Ralph, they were approached by a large whale. The animal surfaced nearby, regarded them with a wary eye, then suddenly submerged and swam beneath their boat. It could have surfaced beneath them, overturning their vessel and throwing them into the sea. They didn't know what to expect next, but were deathly afraid the whale might attack and sink them. Although unusual, it was a possibility. They stood on deck holding each other tight, telling each other that if this were the end, they loved each other dearly and were glad they had had their life together. The whale surfaced next to them and began to rub against the hull of their boat. They waited for what they thought was the inevitable. The whale exhaled a fishy odorous breath through its blowhole, and as they continued to sail, kept pace with them, rubbing against the side of their craft. Then the whale sounded, and was gone. The couple said they nearly fainted from relief once they were certain the animal had departed. Exhausted by their ordeal, the couple soon disappeared below decks.

They were still apparently asleep when Ralph and Alice weighed anchor next morning to get an early start. As they motored past the other craft, Alice recalled the story Ralph repeated to her and Melanie the previous evening. She almost envied the older couple their ordeal because it led to such a powerful declaration of love between them. She doubted that if she and Ralph were ever in extremis upon the sea, they would be embraced in love when the end came.

# Ralph

Everything seemed to be going so well—maybe it seemed too quiet to me because we weren't arguing about anything— that I began to wonder if Alice was really as satisfied as I was with our life together. But it seemed she wasn't, because she decided to go to graduate school to complete her education so she could get herself a better job afterwards. I have to admit that going back to school had helped her find better jobs, but there had to be an end to this. When was she going to just go to work, and stop trying to escape the real world?

So far, she hadn't met anyone else, but somehow I knew that this time it was going to mean trouble for me. I said something to her but she put me off with her usual argument about wanting to do her best for both of us, and our future years, especially when we hit retirement. Perhaps I should have tried harder to tell her how concerned I was, but she was so determined to do it, maybe what I felt about it didn't matter that much to her any more.

By this time, my father would have killed me if I had tried to hold her back from anything she wanted to do. In spite of the political arguments he persisted in instigating with Alice, Dad really did appreciate her. He thought she was brilliant. He believed in education just as much as she did, and he always encouraged her when she wanted to get another degree. He probably thought that I didn't deserve her. He may have been right. I don't know. Alice thought my dad was a real old time pain in the ass, although he could have his redeeming moments. She never said it, but I know that's how she felt about him. Alice hated those political arguments and tried her best to avoid them. Dad was always invigorated by confrontation but over the years he had lost his finesse and now, whether or not he was making any sense, he always shouted her down. That could get pretty loud. So when the two of them clashed, it was more spectacular than ever.

Someone had to keep supporting the family, and it was always me. I just kept doing what Alice expected of me, and no one seemed to notice. I know that things like having a roof over her head and food on the table were important to her. It isn't that she didn't recognize what I contributed to support the family, but while Alice always got lots of attention by doing whatever she did, I got left in the background and was taken for granted.

\*\*\*

At the end of her first year in grad school, Alice had to have surgery. She literally had to be taken from the classroom to the operating room. One of her student friends had called her doctor and then called a cab to rush her to the Emergency Room. She was in pain because of a tumor, and bleeding almost all of the time, but she had been determined to hang in and finish the semester. She just barely made it. The timing was perfect to mess up my plans. I have to admit I was pretty bitter. I knew it was not her fault. I guess I felt strongly that in general, her priorities should have been more tuned to my needs. It was weird to feel that way—it was obvious she couldn't actually control her illness to fit my schedule.

Alice was still in the hospital on the weekend that she and I were supposed to take the boat to Maine for an early charter. Alice was easy to sail with. She always knew what had to be done, and when, so between us we barely had to talk about it.

But of course, she was still lying in a hospital bed recovering from her surgery. We convinced Melanie, the reluctant sailor, to go with me and help deliver the boat in Maine. Melanie hated the idea but she's a good kid and knew how much we needed her to help us out. So she gathered up her favorite CD's, her headphones and the portable player along with enough clothes to change outfits every five minutes—at least it looked that way to me—and we set off.

All the first day it was hot and calm, so we motored, putting in to Cape Ann early in the evening. I went ashore to poke around in the chandlery and while I was there, decided to have a drink at the bar. A good-looking blond came over to me and we struck up a conversation. I invited her back to the boat for a drink and she came. I had forgotten all about Melanie being on board. When Melanie heard two sets of feet step onto the deck, and looked out of the hatch to see who was there, I wished I had decided to single-hand the boat, even all that distance. She took one look at me and the blond and burst out, "Mom's in the hospital. She just had surgery. Do you think this is the way you should be behaving? Do you think you should go out picking up women and bringing them home to your teen-aged daughter?" The blond couldn't get off the boat fast enough.

"Please don't tell your mother. I wasn't trying to pick that woman up," I pleaded with my angry daughter. "She'd never understand."

"Well that makes two of us," Melanie shouted, bursting into tears and disappearing below.

# Alice

On the first day of her graduate school classes, Alice met Brad while standing in line in the cafeteria to buy lunch. He was an older man, not exactly what she thought of as handsome, but good-looking in his own way. Medium brown hair, blue eyes and a diffident smile made a favorable first impression on her. They made their way to the same table. Chatting about their courses, they struck up a friendship that was initially based on shared interests, and then grew over the next few months into something much more. Brad was thoughtful of her and treated her with respect. Alice was unused to a man who would think of her with such sensitivity and it bowled her over. He won her heart. Without realizing it, they paired off; soon the other students began to think of them as a couple.

Brad shared his life with Alice, and she reciprocated. Born on a small ranch in Wyoming, he grew up accustomed to rigorous outdoor work. He attended a small rural school and then headed for California where he enrolled at University of California at Berkeley. After two years of mechanical engineering studies, Brad was recruited into the Marine Corps and served in Vietnam. He tended to not share those experiences with Alice. He felt enough had been reported about the war on the news networks, including much that didn't bear repeating. After signing on for a second tour of duty, he was wounded in a deadly firefight. Awaiting evacuation to a military hospital in Hawaii, Brad was interviewed by a prominent reporter. When his parents saw the brief clip on the evening news, they had been terrified but proud of his determination to serve his country. Seeing their wounded son on television, waiting with a group of soldiers for their flight to the hospital, nearly devastated them. Neighbors and friends called to congratulate them about Brad's few moments of fame on the national news. His parents confined themselves to voicing their pride in him, never articulating their fear for his safe return.

At the end of his rotation, Brad returned home to the U.S. and went back to live at the family ranch. He worked there for a year before claiming his veteran's rights and returning to college to finish his undergraduate engineering degree. After graduation, Brad and a few of his friends found work across the border in the gas fields of Alberta. From there he had moved on to Prudhoe Bay, spending a year on one of the offshore rigs. He decided that he was getting too old for outdoor physical work; because his goal was a career in developing energy resources in Canada or Alaska, he believed he needed to earn his MBA to give him entry to management with one of the large oil and gas companies.

Compared to her own life's odyssey, Alice felt she had lived a much less colorful and dangerous existence. But the facts of her life seemed equally exotic and entrancing to Brad. And so as the months progressed, Brad and Alice drew closer together. He planned to return to Wyoming for the summer, but as the time approached, he began to hesitate in that decision.

When she was not with him, Brad was constantly on Alice's mind. She did not look forward to the several months when she would be without his companionship. On top of everything else, Alice had become ill with a tumor that was rapidly growing inside her. Although benign, the doctor wanted her to have it removed as soon as possible. She delayed long enough so that she could complete her first year of grad school, and then spend two days with Brad before he left for the summer.

Alice had told Ralph she had two days of exams, and went off the first morning as if she were headed for school. She met Brad at the usual coffee shop, at the usual hour. Other students who did have final exams to write were still claiming their same tables. As the room began to empty, Brad asked Alice what she would like to do for the day. They took the train into Boston and walked the narrow streets of Beacon Hill, not saying much to each other. Later in the morning they stopped for coffee at a "greasy spoon" behind the State House. As they walked down Beacon Street, Alice suddenly halted. She turned to Brad and asked in a wavering voice, "Do you really have to go?"

"I've been asking myself that same question for the past month," he sighed. "I don't know that I do, but on the other hand, I told the family to expect me to work on the ranch over the summer. An extra hand will be a big help to them."

"Could you just not be away for such a long time? I'm going to miss you terribly."

"And I'll miss you as well. But you are scheduled for surgery the day after tomorrow. Then you'll have to stay home for six weeks until you recover from it. I can't just show up at your house to visit you, you know. Besides, it would probably drive me crazy to see you in a nightgown when I couldn't put my hands on you." He laughed. "I doubt Ralph would take that very well."

Alice smiled. "It would be hard for me to see you and not be able to reach out to you as well."

Brad pulled her around to him and kissed her. Alice's head was reeling. She didn't move and he kept his arm around her to steady her. "You've walked around quite enough. We'll go to my apartment. You can sit down and put your feet up for a while. We don't have to act like a couple of nomads who have no place to go."

After walking a few more blocks, with Brad mostly supporting Alice, they came to the brownstone where he had a second floor apartment. They entered the building and walked up the flight of stairs. Brad opened the door, revealing the entry into a comfortable sitting area. Alice fell into the nearest chair. "I couldn't have walked any farther," she admitted ruefully. "This isn't the way I am."

He went to the small kitchen and made a cup of tea for her. As they sat there, Alice sipping the hot brew and recovering from the morning, Brad asked if she'd like some Chinese food for lunch. He would call the restaurant and have them deliver it so they wouldn't have to go out again. When she lifted her face in agreement, he leaned down, brushing his lips against hers, then walked into the kitchen to pick up the phone.

She began to feel panicky. "What am I doing here?" Alice thought. "I'm a married woman. I can't have an affair with him."

As if reading her mind, Brad called to her, "You're the first woman I've let in this door. I'm not used to bringing anyone home. This is not something I've ever done before."

Alice replied, "I never took you for a womanizer."

Brad smiled at her. "I must be in love. Why else would I be doing this?" His voice became plummy, making it sound as if he were trying to modify his Midwestern intonation to resemble a British accent.

Alice laughed at his affected tone. "I'm feeling lightheaded. I just need something to eat. Then I'll be fine. I'm not used to so much thoughtfulness. It's nice."

Concerned, Brad came to her side. "Are you comfortable there? Can I get you another pillow? Would you rather lie down? Do you hurt?"

"Maybe I'll lie down and rest until the food comes."

He dialed the phone and placed the order. "It'll be about a half hour. Why don't you try to nap?"

Brad sat beside the bed, leaning forward to gently stroke her arm.

"That's soothing. Tell me about the ranch and what you'll be doing this summer."

After a few sentences, he noticed that she had nodded off. He pulled a throw over her shoulders and left her to rest. When the doorbell rang, she gave a start and opened her eyes. The smell of the Chinese food soon permeated the apartment. Brad put everything out on the table and asked if she felt well enough to sit up and eat something. He regarded her with concern. Her skin was pallid and she looked ill.

"I'm fine. I can sit at the table with you." But she could not sit upright and she could eat nothing.

"What's your doctor's name and phone number? Let's get you into the hospital today. It's closer for you to go from here instead of returning home and then having to come back into the city."

He dialed the phone for her. Dr. Abram told her to get to the emergency room as soon as possible and he would meet her there. Brad called a cab. They left the apartment, their untouched feast cooling on the kitchen table.

"I'll come to visit you once you're settled in. I'll be happier once this is over for you. I have to leave for Wyoming in a couple of days but I will be back." He rattled on as the cab swung in and out of the city traffic, speeding them to the hospital.

Alice's surgery was quickly over, and by that evening she was wheeled from the recovery room into a hospital room in the ward. Brad was true to his word, showing up early the following afternoon, just as visiting hours began. He didn't stay long, and narrowly missed her father-in-law when he left. A red rose remained on the bedside table to remind her of his presence. A few days later she was able to go home from the hospital, the rose pressed between the covers of a novel brought in by a friend.

As she spent the prescribed time recovering at home, with little or nothing to do during her convalescence, she pondered her relationship with Brad. He managed to call her a few times over the summer to ask how she was doing and tell her about his daily adventures on the ranch. He sounded so happy and enthusiastic it emphasized to Alice that she was stuck in a backwater in a holding pattern. Would she ever have as much joy as he in whatever she would end up doing in her life? She was a little envious of his freedom. She asked herself over and over what she should do about Brad. Anyone who has ever experienced hunger for food or for love never forgets how that feels. She longed for him, and felt a void in her soul that might never be filled unless by him. This could bring about the end of her marriage to Ralph. What would she do if Brad asked her to leave Ralph? She didn't know. There was nothing left between her and Ralph. Why should she stay with him? But Alice had to think of her daughter. Melanie was still young. How could she hurt either her adolescent daughter or her unsuspecting husband? Whenever her thoughts turned in that direction, guilt threatened to overwhelm her. Then her eyes would water and her face streak with tears.

*\*\**

At the end of the summer, Brad called to tell her he was back in town. The new semester would begin in a couple of weeks. How soon could he see her?

"I have to get my books," she told him. "When can we meet? I'll plan to come into the city then. This will be my first trip in since the day you rushed me to the hospital in that kamikaze cab. This time I'll drive myself in there. By the time I finish getting textbooks, I'll have too much to carry to be able to take everything home on the train. I'm not quite back to being anywhere near strong enough to carry a real armload."

"Oh come on, Alice," Brad chided her. "It's been years since I've carried books for a girl. But if I were going to do that, you'd be who I'd do it for. Just think of me as your own private pack mule."

She chuckled, "You're back all right, along with your unique sense of humor. I've missed you."

The next day they met and went together to the bookstore. They piled their textbooks into her car, had lunch, and then drove to Brad's apartment. They unloaded his books and sat talking.

Alice realized that he had missed her as much as she had missed him. He leaned over to kiss her forehead, then sat down beside her and pulled her to him. As they held each other in a close embrace, he touched her face and asked, "Have you recovered from your surgery? Are you all right now?"

"I think so," she responded, gazing fondly at him. She was

content, feeling his arms around her and the warmth of his body. He held her gently.

"Alice, I want you so much that I can hardly bear it, but I don't want to hurt you." He kissed her lightly on the lips and then kissed the side of her face.

"I want you too, Brad. I have done nothing but think about you all summer. I've waited for you to come back. I've hoped for this moment and been uneasy about it, too."

"My dearest Alice, I cannot imagine my life going on without you." It all seemed to flow so naturally, even that endearing awkwardness that comes of being first-time lovers. He guided her gently toward the bedroom. "Is there anything you need?"

"Only you," she responded, embracing him. He began to slowly unbutton her blouse, stroking her hair and face as he did so. She slowly helped him remove his tee shirt. He held her gently against his bare chest, stroking her throat with his thumb, his fingers curled about her slender neck. His hand then moved slowly to her breasts and he kissed the warm surface of her skin.

His voice caught as he whispered, "Sweetheart, I love you." That sent goose bumps down her spine. She shivered. They stood, a long kiss ending in a contented sigh, his hands cupping her breasts. Their bodies pressed together, and then parted just enough to sink down onto the bed. For a long time neither spoke. Finally they lay quietly in each other's arms. For the first time in her life, she felt like this was the way lovemaking was supposed to be.

*** 

Alice found it difficult to juggle her classes, assignments, exams, daughter, husband, and love affair. Once the semester began it was hard for them to find time to be together in his apartment. Alice had a long commute in and out of the city, and was exhausted by the time she got home in the evening, to take up her family's daily needs.

One beautiful Indian summer day in early October as they rested in Brad's bed after making love, they lay together near a window that framed a glorious golden maple tree. The afternoon sun shone through the leaves illuminating them in gold. Rosy skin suffused in golden light, they could have been the motif for Adam and Eve in an illuminated manuscript.

The year progressed to winter, and in the spring as the first flowers broke through the frosted soil, Brad became increasingly importunate with Alice to divorce Ralph. Alice managed to avoid the topic during the dark days of winter, but now the increasing light and warmth of the waxing season illuminated not only the awakening of earthly life, but the inner landscape of their relationship as well. Alice had to face up to the situation. Melanie was not yet an adult in the eyes of the law. A divorce would surely entail a lengthy legal battle. If her daughter had to choose one parent over the other, which would it be? Was it worth putting them all through that, or would it be better to wait a couple of years until Melanie had come of age? If she left Ralph now, she was afraid he could get custody of their daughter. If so, what would be her relationship with Melanie for the rest of their lives? She felt it was an evil choice—that of Melanie, or Brad. She dared not risk it.

As the academic year moved to its close, graduation looming near, Brad was offered a job that would take him back to the gas fields of Alberta. He would have a management position in a large energy company expanding operations into the Arctic. He would leave within the week, not waiting for graduation ceremonies. The opportunity seemed perfect for him. He discussed it with Alice, hesitating as she expressed her fears. A divorce was one thing, and Alice was certainly willing to leave Ralph. But for the next couple of years there would be the added concern of Melanie. Would Alice be able to take her across an international border while she was seeking to divorce Ralph? Alice felt overwhelmed. After all their talking and lovemaking, everything came down to Alice not being able to leave her daughter behind.

"No mother could do that," she was adamant. "Besides, legally she's almost an adult. Can we wait a couple of years to be together? Then the time would be right. We can travel to see each other meanwhile. But by then, Melanie will be of age, ready to take hold of her own life, and she won't need me as a constant presence. Then I could do it wholeheartedly."

After one especially agonizing afternoon, followed by a second, and then a third, Alice finally convinced Brad that she couldn't leave her daughter to go with him right now. She would do it in two years' time. She would count the days until they could be together again. When that happened, it would be for the rest of their lives. Weeping, and clasping him to her, Alice told Brad, "You are my only love. My life would never be the same without you." She didn't know if she would recover from separating from him. Brad was her soul mate. He held her tightly to him, tears running down his face. The pain of separation was almost beyond their endurance. Together or apart, the power of their love would bind and unite them in a single spirit.

"I'll write to you. I'll wait for you, Alice. Whatever it takes, we will be together, even if it takes a while. Nothing lasts forever. We're both adults with other responsibilities that need to be worked out and this gives us the time to do that. It wouldn't be right for me to expect you to leave your daughter behind and run off with me. I couldn't do that to you."

A day later, she met him at the airport, stood with him at the gate when his flight was called, kissed him tearfully, and then remained in the lounge watching the plane back away from the gate and take its place in line for the take-off. It finally lunged skyward, headed for Calgary. It might as well have been headed halfway around the world; his destination seemed that remote to her. Blinded by tears, Alice walked toward the exit. She would be reunited with Brad in two years, that is, if they managed to survive this parting. Then Alice's world fell to pieces. She descended into a deep depression. Her lover was gone, and she could barely function without him.

# Ralph

Once Alice finished her graduate work, it was time for her to become a full time working professional. I was delighted that she would cease this everlasting going back to school. Melanie was the one we should be worried about. But one thing I have to give her, Alice earned her own way. Her extended college work didn't cost me anything.

Just before graduation, Alice and some of her student friends got together to celebrate. There was the usual stuff, booze and marijuana. There were mostly female students at the party, and those girls pulled out all the stops. I remember one very striking girl, a blond. What a beauty she was! How could any man who saw her ever forget her? She was wearing one of those clingy knit dresses with a scooped neckline and no underwear. That was obvious to anyone who even glanced in her direction. Her face was flushed and her erect nipples thrust beneath the material stretched across her proud bare breasts. She was athletically thin, well-muscled and had a flat stomach. The dress was stretched so tightly around her body that even the mound of her pubic hair showed through the fabric that wrapped around her pelvis. I felt my body responding even before she brushed up against me, excusing herself while trying to squeeze past, her tits rubbing across my chest. Did she do that on purpose? It was the first time in my life I had ever been conscious of the potency of female pheromones. It overpowered me. All I could feel was desire. My body glowed with the heat. I had to have her. She seemed pretty high. All I could think of after that was I might have a chance if there was a place where we could be alone for just long enough. The feeling was so strong that it was as if there was only her and me, and everyone else had just faded away as if they never even existed. Primal lust expanded my manhood. I had never felt this way about my wife.

Suddenly Alice came around the corner, took one look at me and said we really should leave as we had an early morning if we were going to be on time for the graduation ceremony. That was that. I wondered if one of the other girls had snitched and told Alice something was going on. Her face seemed red and a little teary. I never dared to ask her that straight out.

Driving home that night and every time I thought about it afterward, I was shocked this could have happened to me, and so fast. It was like being struck by lightning. In the car, Alice said to me, "I trust you, Ralph, but I don't trust all those good-looking single women." After that we drove along in silence. I started to think about the party again. Every other person seemed to have been smoking a joint in that room where that girl appeared. Should I have taken that drag? Had I inhaled too much? I couldn't believe the way it had hit me. One of the guys I knew that was a recreational smoker kept telling me that I should try it because it made everything seem so vivid, and released all inhibitions. He said it was incredible how fast it could happen. Now I believed it.

What I was expecting Alice to do was yell at me all the way home for trying to corner the young lady. She must have known about it, but she never brought it up. I thought about it a lot afterward, but I could never figure out why she didn't pick a fight with me right then in the car. Sometimes I would think, "Nah, she didn't realize I was trying to make her friend Betty. And Betty was too high to remember me. Even if she did recall what happened at the party, she wouldn't tell on me because she'd be too afraid of hurting Alice's feelings." After that, I decided I had to watch myself and be a lot more careful.

\*\*\*

The following year, Melanie graduated from high school and got early acceptance at a school in New York State. Just at about that time, with Melanie gone off to school, Alice fell into a depression for no reason that I could see. At first, I asked her to talk to me about it, but she wouldn't. Then I suggested she try a counselor. I couldn't believe she took Melanie's leaving so hard but then maybe it was just the empty nest syndrome or something. She was pretty touchy and it didn't take much to set her off. Sometimes it kind of felt like she might be looking at me and measuring me against someone else. I quickly let go of that thought. I was persistent and finally, she told me one night after I asked her yet again, "Alice, what's the matter with you? You're not yourself. I just want to help if I can. Is it Melanie?" She went upstairs to the bedroom. I followed her. She lay on the bed crying. I had a sudden flash of instinct, and asked her, "Is there another man?"

She stopped sobbing, sat up, wiped her nose and turned to me, "Yes." That was all she said.

I was off on a tirade, yelling at her. "What's the matter with me? What's the matter with us? Why don't you love me? Why? Why? Why?" I shouted, pounding the mattress. She was frightened now. She jumped up and ran downstairs. I yelled at her, "What are you doing? Where do you think you're going?" She stood in the doorway, turned to face me, and confessed to having an affair. It was over because her lover had died in plane crash. What does that mean? Had she been planning to leave me and go with him? I didn't know if I could ever forgive her. Would she forgive me if she knew about the one-night stands I've had? I thought about that—what I had to forgive her for, and what she might have to forgive me for if she knew about it. Maybe that made us even, I don't know. But in that moment, I decided to ask her if she wanted to make a new start. Either our marriage was going to come apart at the seams, or we'd try our best to hold things together. Finally, as we talked about that, we calmed down. Alice agreed she would give it her best effort. She felt she owed me that much.

"Ralph, if we really try, things can be better than they were before. Think of Melanie," she insisted. I thought we could try. If it didn't work out, we wouldn't be any worse off than we already were. But then, when I started thinking about it, I wasn't sure that I wanted her to make any effort at all. I thought that I might like my freedom. But we'd try. We had promised that to each other—that we'd make the effort.

\*\*\*

Alice started talking about moving to a smaller place, selling the antique house, which neither one of us had enough time to keep up with anymore, and the boat, which was getting to be more expensive and time-consuming than we first expected. They were symbols of how we had lived in the past and she said she didn't want any more association with them. They were too loaded with unhappy memories. We needed a fresh start. We could consolidate what we had invested in both that house and the boat into a single smaller home. Alice made her pitch so often that she got to be quite persuasive. Finally, I gave in to her.

One Sunday she held up the real estate section of the paper, waving it at me across the room. She said she was interested in looking at some houses being built on the harbor. I was willing to at least go with her to look and see if that was something that would work for us. Wouldn't you know it? Before long, we found the perfect place, a very expensive house right on the waterfront. It was five times the very low mortgage payment left on the antique. Alice pointed out that I was now making five times the salary I had been making when we bought the house twenty years earlier, and without the boat to pay for as well, we would be in fine shape to carry the mortgage on the new place. It would also be perfect for retirement. By that time it would be all paid for.

After we had lived there for a year, I thought we could afford a smaller boat. Our marriage was still under re-construction and maybe this would help. So after we talked about it and spent some time looking, we finally found one we both liked. We would keep the boat where we could see it from the window of our living room; it wouldn't have to be chartered to support itself. We could take it wherever we wanted to go, and use it whenever we wanted instead of having to tuck in the odd weekend between charters. It sounded so much easier than what we had done before. Maybe we would be able to relax more with each other. Who knows? Maybe this could work out for us. We decided to give it a try.

Then Melanie dropped out of college, moved into her own apartment and went to work. She was still thinking about going back to school for barn management, somewhere in Pennsylvania or West Virginia. She had always loved horses; she took as many riding lessons as possible during her teen years. Girls seemed to be like that; at least, a lot of her friends were. So long as she could figure out how to manage it, good for her. Alice paid her own tuition, and I made sure Melanie was reminded of that. If she paid for it, she'd take it seriously instead of this start and stop stuff she had been doing when I was paying tuition for her.

For a while, things were good. I was glad that I didn't have to depend on Alice's income to help out because she started one job, then left to take another, then got laid off, and spent a year doing a little—very little—consulting. She finally got a really good job, one that was very demanding. The times she had to be on call were sometimes more strenuous than her regular work week. She was always tired and wasn't much fun to be around any more. She was distracted, as they say.

Because we never talked about things like that between us, I assumed Alice was okay with me finding outlets with other women. Well, after all, men need to have sex more than women do and it is almost the same as getting permission, isn't it?

# Alice

After Brad left, Alice had a very difficult time pulling herself back together. She had no enthusiasm for anything and took her time job-hunting. She walked the beach nearly every day, thinking about Brad and whether her decision had been the right one. He wrote to her at once to let her know where he was, and that he had settled into a very fast-paced environment. He loved it, but missed her tremendously. He wanted her to join him. She wrote back that for the moment that would be impossible. She loved him, missed him terribly, and again asked him to wait for her.

Later in the year, Alice found a new job. She traveled and met a host of people who soon befriended her. She felt like she was accomplishing something and she began to feel her depression receding. Letters from Brad were excited and upbeat. She began to correspond with him in the same tone. He was pleased to see the change, and encouraged her. He always expressed the hope it would not be long before she could join him. Melanie would graduate soon. Once she was off to college, Alice could raise the issue of a divorce with Ralph.

During the summer following Melanie's graduation, Alice received a stunning letter from Brad's parents. He had told them everything about his relationship with Alice and that he planned to marry her once she would be free. They had hoped to meet her soon, but now that was unlikely.

Brad's mother Mary wrote, "Brad was asked to travel out to an oil rig in the North Sea. Because of his early experience at Prudhoe Bay and his current management responsibilities, he was the only one the company could send to do the job. Workers on the platform had raised some issues about the rig's safety equipment. Brad was sent to investigate. He flew to London and was taken to the rig by helicopter. The mission went well, but as they were flying back to Heathrow for Brad's return to Canada, something went wrong with one of the helicopter rotors. The pilot radioed a distress call saying something about a heavy wind gust disabling the rear rotor, and high seas below them, just before the craft went down. The open mike transmitted the sounds of men shouting. Then there was the thump of an impact, followed by silence. The search for survivors ended with the recovery of some of the bodies of the men who had been on board. Brad's remains were identified. They flew his body home to Wyoming. The family had his remains cremated, and we all said farewell to him as we scattered his ashes from the highest point on the ranch. We're going to place a marker on the site.

"Alice, I know how hard a blow this will be for you. I can hardly bear the burden myself, but I wanted to be the one to let you know of his death. I am sorry for all of us who loved him. As much as we have been shocked and horrified at the manner of losing him, we know that the love you shared with our son must leave you as bereft as we are. Please think of us as your family. We looked forward to you and Brad marrying. You were the only one that was ever so deeply embedded in his heart. Bless you, my dear."

Brad's untimely death overwhelmed her. Alice was devastated. She wept for days after she received Mary's letter. She folded it up and hid it inside her bureau along with the stack of Brad's letters, taking it out to read it a second, and then a third time. Each new reading brought a fresh stab of pain. She wanted to die. She wished she had gone with him even to have such a little time together. Maybe she could have prevented his being sent on that errand to the North Sea. Any company would rather send a single man on such a dangerous assignment than a married man. If she had only been with him, maybe he would not have had to go. Did he think of her in his last moments? She plummeted to the depths of her grief. It encased her heart. Mechanically she plodded through one day, then another.

Ralph persisted in trying to learn what was wrong with her. When Alice succumbed to his importuning in a moment of deep sorrow and confessed her relationship with Brad, he exploded in anger. She sank into an even deeper chasm of anguish. He wrung a promise from her to work on restoring their marriage for their daughter's sake. Afterward he seemed to drift away from her again.

*** 

Alice needed a ceremony, however private, to acknowledge Brad's death. That was long overdue. Without it she would always be stuck in the place of believing he was still alive, off somewhere in the world doing important things, not yet ready to return to her. His letters had long since ceased, the last one arriving a week after his death. That was written while he was still out on the rig. When she read it, her heart had broken all over again.

One day she took a lunchtime harbor cruise, boarding the boat with an enormous bouquet of flowers. Passing the harbor islands, she stood in the stern of the boat and dropped the blossoms into its wake, where they bobbed like so many pieces of confetti. Above her in the wheelhouse, a member of the crew watched. He had seen this sort of thing before. Usually, if it were a man or woman, a single red rose would be discretely dropped overboard. Families usually brought bouquets. A child would send one over with a single toss. An adult would drop a bouquet flower by flower, as if remembering significant moments with the loved one who had now been lost. But she stood there with the largest armful of flowers he had yet seen, enough to be the whole inventory of one of the local vendors. He wondered at the link people seemed to make between water and eternity. Each toss he had witnessed in his years of working on this vessel spoke to that connection. Whatever it was, it seemed to bring them some spiritual good. He watched Alice for a few minutes, and could see her lips moving as she prepared to drop the next blossom. He wished her peace and returned to his task.

Alice's heart spoke to her dead lover. "These are for you, Brad, my only love, for all that we had and all that we might have had. I need to think of you scattering blessings on all of us you've left behind, just as I'm scattering these flowers in memory of you." A breath of air blew against her cheek. It felt to her like his kiss. "You are there, I know it. You'll never leave me. I will always love you." At the end of the cruise, she left the boat, her heart and her burden of sorrow lighter, a wan smile on her face.

Soon afterward, Alice wrote to Brad's mother to tell her about it, and about how she was now beginning to feel some resolution about his death. She said she had suffered his loss greatly. Now she believed she was ready to try to pull herself together and go on with her life. She still felt hesitant about her ability to succeed, but she must do so, for the sake of her sanity. Mary had immediately responded with a letter of her own.

"Dearest Alice,

It has been the hardest thing in my life to accept that my child has gone before me. It was devastating for me, to think that all that bright promise, the love we all have for him, and the hope for his happiness with you, were dashed in a few brief moments of violent impact. Writing those few words still has the power to bring tears to my eyes.

Before we took his ashes to scatter, I saved some in a small urn which I keep on my dresser. I see him every time I look at it, and think about his life. But I share with you the need to let go of him, as you must have felt while scattering the flowers, and as I had watching his ashes disperse into the air. We all needed a ceremonial parting. My family provided mine and now you have had your own. I think it helped you in mourning Brad.

Perhaps you wrote to me because you found that it was only a temporary resolution of your sorrow in losing him. It was still an important step along the route of accepting that this wonderful person is lost to us forever, and of finally absorbing that pain. But I think neither of us has quite finished letting go of him.

At some time in the future, when you can do so, we would love for you to come to the ranch. Then you can see his marker, a wonderful stone set on a hillside, and together you and I can scatter the rest of his remains. I will keep those until you come. No matter what, Alice, we will always welcome you here. With all my love, Mary."

Alice felt blessed by Mary's letter and her invitation, and sent a note saying how much she appreciated both. Yes, Alice told her, I shall come but don't know when that may be possible.

Now she would make her best effort with Ralph. She had promised him that after her confession to him. They shared a child. But in her heart, Alice knew she would never deny her love for Brad.

*\*\*\**

They moved to the harbor. It was spring. The days were warm, and the views out over the water were beautiful. Alice had high hopes that in this place, without a lot of conflicting responsibilities, their marriage would have the best chance to rekindle and blossom anew. One somber note intruded in this hopeful reverie. As their new home had neared completion, there was an encounter with one of the carpenters. The man was well-intentioned. He rhapsodized about the beauty of the place and how romantic it would be to live there.

"I'll sell it to you," Ralph snarled.

Alice, caught off guard, blanched and shrank back from the venom in his voice. Flustered, the carpenter pursued his point, "A lot of guys would love to live in a place like this with their wives. I would love to live in a place like this with my girl-friend." By the end of his brief, well-intentioned speech, the man's face was beet red.

Ralph never hesitated. "I said I'd sell it to you. It's too expensive for me and I cannot afford it."

Alice turned away in tears. "You pay for it. You were the one who wanted this place," he shouted at her. The venom and anger of that moment never completely passed. Its lingering presence set the tone for the balance of their married life.

\*\*\*

Alice recalled that when they were dating, Ralph had said something about moving on. She had spontaneously cried out to him, "You are very generous with your money but you are not at all generous with your self."

If Alice had only realized at that insightful moment how well she had pegged Ralph, she might have found the nerve to let him go right then and there. What was wrong with her on that occasion?

Ralph had responded by breaking into tears and hugging Alice closer to him. "You're right. I have to change that."

She believed that he wanted to change, that he could and that he would make the effort to do so. Trusting him, she continued to date him. Not too long after that episode came the afternoon when her fate was sealed. Now she had agreed to trust him once again, in his promise that he would try with her to re-establish their marriage. Was he any more capable now of changing than he had been all those years ago?

\*\*\*

By the end of their first year of living on the harbor, Ralph itched to get back out on the water. He decided they could afford to have a boat after all, smaller than the one they had just had, but they would be able to keep it for their own use. They talked a lot about making another commitment to boating. Alice wanted to cruise the coast as they had in earlier years as new sailors. Her work now took all of her energy during the week. She sought relaxation rather than excitement. Ralph seemed enthusiastic about that, and so they took their time to find just the right vessel. It was like a small vacation to travel to the Chesapeake on their mission. It was a refreshing interlude, and left them on a high note when it ended.

They no longer expected that Melanie would ever sail with them again, so they sought a vessel that would accommodate both of them comfortably, and allow occasional visitors to spend a weekend on board. Finally they found a smaller ketch that seemed to suit them both. A spacious open cockpit where they could sit and enjoy themselves, comfortable living space below, combined with sturdy construction and beautiful classic lines appealed to them. They were able to negotiate a reasonable price for the craft. They would travel to take possession of the boat and then sail it home. They had done that before, and would use it as an excuse to take some vacation time from work. They'd make their leisurely way along the coast to enjoy themselves, unwind a little while getting to know the boat, and possibly even get back in touch with each other. It sounded perfect.

*** 

Replete with challenges, the journey was anything but what they anticipated. The pleasurable part ended on the second day when the engine belched black smoke as Ralph tried to start it up while they were sailing across Vineyard Sound. They managed to make their way into a nearby cove where Ralph spent the rest of the day with a phalanx of tools spread out across the cockpit seats, working on the boat's small diesel. Once that was repaired, they set out to cross Buzzards Bay and transit the Cape Cod Canal. As they entered the west end of the Canal, smoke spewed forth once more, and they pulled into a small anchorage so Ralph could perform another miracle with the contents of his toolkit. Once again underway, everything seemed in order. Still at a distance from home, and keyed up to expect anything to cut loose at any moment, both were tense and nervous.

When they were approaching home waters and feeling like they might make it back without further excitement, the steering gears popped out. They made their run up the channel and into the harbor with Ralph in the bilge holding things in place and Alice at the wheel. They sailed toward their mooring through a swarm of other boats. This time their luck held. There was no one using their mooring and they picked it up on the first pass. They were home. Alice shed a few tears of relief that this inauspicious first voyage was indeed over. Ralph was furious.

***

During the next couple of years, Alice went less often to the boatyard during spring and fall weekends, while Ralph spent more time there. Alice's professional life now completely engaged her. Ralph seemed happy enough. Both appeared in better harmony with each other. Beneath the veneer there was no real connection. They might have been a brother and sister living in accord and simply sharing a residence, rather than husband and wife.

When Ralph finally came home at night after work, his main interest was whatever was on television. Other than the mechanical responses each made to the question "How was your day?" or to share news of Melanie, there were few topics of conversation that were of mutual concern.

Alice would go upstairs early, and fall asleep reading. Ralph would fall asleep in front of the TV and crawl quietly into bed in the wee hours of the morning. Alice rose early to get to work on time. Ralph's flexible schedule meant that he did not often appear until Alice was nearly ready to leave. They passed in the doorway, coming and going. That passage was the most intimate part of their day.

Ralph claimed to have lost interest in Alice as her involvements expanded well beyond the house and the boat. "You bore me," he told her one day, apropos of nothing. Alice's reaction was one of shock and concern. She knew she had tried to make things work, but now it seemed that had likely been a vain expectation. She wondered how much longer she could go on this way. By then, Ralph was not hiding the fact that he found other women a lot more exciting than the one he had married all those years ago.

*** 

Their routine was abruptly shattered when Melanie was taken to the hospital one night after what appeared to be a suicide attempt. She dialed 911 and then called her boyfriend Stan. He arrived just moments ahead of the police.

The phone rang at dinnertime. Alice expected it was Ralph calling yet again to say he was stopping for a drink with one of his friends at the office before coming home.

Instead, Alice heard the unmistakable Voice of the Law at the other end, calling from The Hospital. "Your daughter is all right but she is being held in restraints. Come as soon as possible." The Voice continued to speak, giving additional information. Alice held the phone, struggling to listen and take it all in, as disbelief clouded her brain. She thought they must have called the wrong number. Then the Voice spoke her name, enunciating each word loudly and clearly, "Alice, I am calling about your daughter Melanie. She's in The Hospital. Get here as soon as you can."

In a rare act of Providence, Ralph chose that very moment to walk in the door. The Voice was still on the phone. Alice told him her husband had just come home, and would he tell Ralph what he just told her? When Ralph took the phone from her, she put their dinners down the garbage disposal, got her coat, and as soon as he hung up they left for the hospital.

After that night, Alice began to consciously live one day at a time. It was the only way she could cope with the ordeal of her daughter's illness. She soon learned to dread a ringing telephone, at home or at the office. It could be a summons for her to drop everything and rush to the hospital for another of Melanie's episodes. Treatment and counseling alternated with the hospitalizations. The disease robbed Melanie of her former vitality and zest for the future. It completely took over her life.

After the first year, Stan, who dearly loved Melanie and had been a pillar of support for her, even moving into her apartment to take care of her, made his tearful exit. During that year his presence shielded Alice and Ralph from the worst of Melanie's troubles, and in doing so Stan suffered more than either parent. Intending they would marry once Melanie stabilized, he lived a life with her that was eloquent in his love and support. A hard worker, Stan put in long hours at his job. Melanie resented his absences, and would sometimes call Alice and complain. Alice understood Melanie's loneliness but also recognized that her illness controlled her actions. Alice tried to walk the line between justifying Stan and appeasing Melanie. Each call became more difficult than the one before.

After Stan parted from her, Melanie either lived at home with Alice and Ralph, or tried to live elsewhere on her own. For a long time, Melanie's living arrangements also included hospitalizations for various intervals. When that happened, Alice and Ralph took turns making visits after work, and then went together to the hospital on weekends. Each time Melanie was released from an extended stay, they were relieved and exhausted. Without noticing it, they fell even farther apart as each tried to salve their own wounds and recoup their own strength for what they knew would sooner or later come again.

Melanie was making a heroic effort to control the urges brought on by the disease. From the beginning, they were overwhelming and frightening. Voices only she could hear either shouted at her or pleaded with her to cut herself. For a while, medication would help, then the voices would break through and the cycle would start up again. It was enervating for Melanie to live with. Her parents were heartbroken.

The constant in Melanie's life was her counselor, Angela, who tried to help Melanie sort out what was happening to her and develop ways to cope with it. The first time that Melanie called 911 and asked to be taken to the hospital because she recognized an episode was about to start, Alice felt there had been a breakthrough. As Melanie gained more control over the disease, the hospitalizations became voluntary.

# Ralph

Our lives changed in an instant. It happened the night that I came home from work at dinnertime and found Alice on the phone with a hospital. They had Melanie. She was injured and in trouble. We had to go immediately. No time to eat dinner, just get in the car and drive to a hospital that was a good hundred miles from us.

When we arrived at the E.R., we were taken to a small room, barely the size of a closet, a guard by the door, where Melanie lay strapped to a hospital bed. She acted like she was out of it. When I said something about what they had used to treat her, the guard said her blood alcohol level was so high they couldn't medicate her, so they had to use restraints to keep her from falling out of the bed. Both of her arms were wrapped in bandages from her wrists to her elbows. She lay there looking completely helpless, but with a crazy, brave grin on her face. What happened to her? We couldn't even begin to imagine.

The story she told us was just plain frightening. She went out for a ride and started drinking. Somewhere along the way, she got an overwhelming urge—voices from deep inside told her to end her life by cutting her wrists. So she got a knife and drove, drinking and cutting herself. Somehow she managed to get home. Once there, she got scared and dialed 911, then called her boyfriend Stan before she passed out. Stan got there just ahead of the cops. They took one look and arrested him for attempted murder. The ambulance took Melanie to the Emergency Room and Stan went with the police. They finally cleared him of any charges just before we got to the hospital.

Stan, Alice and I sat with Melanie in the emergency room all night long. Around midnight, the doctor on duty came over and told us she would be transported in the morning to a mental hospital. They would hold her for three days and possibly longer. Melanie couldn't do it for herself, so with her permission, Alice and I had to sign papers so they could move her. She was our daughter, but she was also an adult in the eyes of the law. This was the first inkling of what that meant in terms of our trying to take care of her, or get any information about her and her condition. We were slow learners. It just seemed to us that as her parents we should have information about what was happening to her and be able to make decisions about her care. We only wanted to help. They had to have her permission first. I found that strange.

Around 3 a.m., I decided that it would be a good thing if we all took a trip to Disneyland for a week of vacation together, after Melanie finished her hospitalization. So we started talking about that—where we would stay, what we would like to do, the rides we'd take, just laughing and letting our imaginations run wild about all the fun and childish things we would do. I thought if she had that to look forward to, Melanie would try her best to get over whatever made her do this to herself. By 4 a.m., we were laughing and talking and really into it, everything we'd do on this vacation. Melanie was pretty upbeat by this time. It'd be great. I'd have a travel agent set it up as soon as Melanie would be ready to take a trip.

Then another doctor came into the room and told us there was an ambulance outside to take Melanie to the next hospital. He told us where it was and said if we wanted, we could follow it. So off we went. It was barely daybreak, the first rosy smudges of light just beginning to brighten the horizon. There wasn't much traffic. The trip was fairly short. We were across the city before we knew it.

In another hospital waiting room, we stood by and watched the nurse on duty help Melanie complete the necessary admission forms. By the time we saw her settled in and were ready to leave, the morning commute was in full swing. We were miles away, from home and from what our lives had been up to that moment on the previous evening when Alice received that phone call. We had to go home, get ready for work, and then we were both going to be late getting to our respective offices. We needed a change of clothes, but more than that we both needed a good night's sleep so we could wake up and find out that this whole thing was nothing more than the worst nightmare we'd ever had.

Unfortunately, it was all too real. We were in for a terrible time. This was just the first of a long string of events in Melanie's illness. This time, after about a week, she left the hospital with some medications, and Stan took her home to her apartment. A month later, we all took the trip to Disney. I hoped that it would be a dividing line that would separate Melanie's future from what had just happened to her. I thought of it as a celebration that she had been sick, but now she was going to get better. No more emergencies. I could not have been more wrong about that. Her illness was just beginning to show itself for the terrifying thing that it was. For several years, she would go in cycles. She would have a crisis and wind up in the hospital. She'd come out with different medications which would work for a while, and then as those lost their effectiveness, there would be another crisis.

Stan lived with her for about a year, then he couldn't take it any more. Who could blame him? It was a tough farewell. He loaded a rental truck with her stuff and brought it all to our house. When he opened the back of the vehicle, everything was jumbled on the floor of the truck bed—including some plants and her childhood collection of Teddy bears—all lying about in chaos, just like our lives had become.

We cried a lot that day. Then we picked up the pieces, of

Melanie's stuff, and of our lives. It would be a long time before we could really be able to connect all this with our daughter, our perfect blond, blue-eyed princess. It would take several more episodes to bring home to us the bare awful fact that this was her life. It scared us to death.

Alice tried joining a support group to get more information about Melanie's diagnosis, which the doctors still weren't exactly certain about. But after several months, she stopped going to meetings because she felt herself going around in circles. She had a hard time relating to some of the others in the group. We were both flailing. We just plain didn't know what to do, but now we knew there would be a "next time" for something to happen in Melanie's illness. We wanted to prevent that, and protect her and us.

After a few years of this, Angela, Melanie's therapist, observed an annual cycle. Melanie would be depressive during the winter, start coming up in the spring, be very high energy in the summer, and descend during the fall to the winter low point. Spring and fall, the times of changing, were the times we really had to watch her. Those were the times that she was most likely to have to be hospitalized.

As her parents, Alice and I were each trying to cope with it in our own way. Alice had a demanding job on top of everything else, but at least it was so local that she could come home for lunch every day. I had to work long hours, and it just got easier for me to come home later and later. Weekends when Alice was cleaning the house and grocery shopping, I would go to the boatyard.

Melanie was living with us again. It seemed she was always watching sitcoms or movies on TV. She had trouble concentrating on anything. She was passing time, trying to cope, to pull herself together, trying not to hear the persistent voices that would start to speak in her head as the medications became less effective. She was trying to work with Angela to find ways to get control of herself so she could go back to living a normal life. It was heartbreaking.

Mercifully, on that first night, we didn't know any of this.

I, at least, thought it would be a one-time thing. I don't know what Alice might have thought that night, or if she even had been able to think enough about it to have any kind of an opinion. We were just plain exhausted and didn't talk much on the way home. Alice decided to call in sick and get some needed sleep. She was pretty wrung out. I couldn't sleep so I told her I had to go to my office for a few hours.

What I did was shower and change into fresh clothes, and then call my girl-friend Bunny. I really needed someone to talk to, but not about this. Bunny was always good to me. I just wanted to lie in her arms and not think about anything but her and me together. I wanted to check the baggage for a while.

# Alice

On the day that her Uncle Ed's Korean War veteran flag was first raised to fly for one month over a war memorial located in his old South Boston neighborhood, Alice's company announced a downsizing, including the termination of her position. Alice was so distracted by Melanie's situation that she never saw it coming. The company announced in one of the large urban newspapers it no longer needed a group of positions. Terminating them would save over a million dollars a year. A list of names including hers was printed in the article that described the cutback. It was a done deal. Cast loose and thrust into searching for work, Alice soon found another position to move on to. It seemed the appropriate metaphor for what she knew she must do to resolve other parts of her life.

Ralph's response to the news was no different than his response to earlier situations when Alice had suffered some important setback. "I have to work to support both of us. I cannot afford to get upset about you and your problems, so I don't want to discuss it. By the way, have you thought about how you're going to manage your car payments and your share of the bills?"

His sister Penelope echoed Ralph's sentiment when she learned of Alice's misfortune. "Who's going to pay for your pretty little car," she snidely remarked when she called to ask Alice how she was doing.

Years of similar reactions to her various plights taught Alice to take them in stride, and not give them any more attention than they deserved. It was uncomfortable, but Alice understood that she would have work only when there were fires to fight and obstacles to overcome. Her new job was to be temporary as well. At least she had one.

\*\*\*

A couple of weeks after the public announcement that Alice's job had been severed, Angela invited her to a meeting of all of Melanie's caregivers. Ralph was unavailable, so she went alone. The medical building looked like a great gray fortress standing close by the highway. Alice heard just what she expected from that group. In their opinion, Alice must go to court and be declared Melanie's guardian and then have her committed to an institution. Otherwise, these concerned professionals told her, they couldn't guarantee that Melanie would survive another five years. Alice felt her face suddenly go gray and her mouth dry. She had nothing to say that they wanted to hear. She offered no automatic concurrence with their opinions. This was too big a step to be lightly or quickly taken. She couldn't do it without consulting her husband. Alice imparted this information with a certain amount of irony. As the meeting ended, she merely thanked them for sharing their information and advice. Exiting the building, Alice fought back her tears.

Angela, trailing behind, called out to her. "What did you think about all that?"

Alice stopped her flight and turned back into the moment. "I really don't know. They're the professionals, so they should know what they're talking about. I just don't feel right about following their advice." After a brief pause, Alice continued, "Most importantly, I can't face the thought of Melanie being confined in some institution and having all the decisions about how to make her own life taken away from her—even temporarily—never mind what I heard them say at that meeting.

Melanie is an adult and would probably fight that. She might even succeed. Or she could just plain run away and disappear. And what would happen to her then? It will take some time to work this out with her, and to convince her that decision—if it ever had to be made—would be provisional and strictly for her own good."

Angela sighed with relief. "I'm glad we're thinking along the same lines. That makes me feel better. What will you do now?" Angela looked anxiously at Alice's ravaged face. The women hugged and Alice silently took her leave.

That evening over dinner, Alice dutifully reported to Ralph on the meeting with Melanie's caregivers and her reaction to it. Melanie was meeting with Angela, and would hear the details from her, before deciding what she wanted to say about it to her parents. Neither of them could imagine Melanie wanted anything other than to be allowed to live her own life to the best of her ability to do so, even if it meant that she could be drawn into other suicide attempts. Both agreed that Melanie might actually take off to avoid being placed in an institution and then what would happen if or when she did make another attempt? Who would be there to help her? The whole idea the caregivers had presented could only succeed if Melanie were locked up immediately, with no possible escape. What a cruel decision that would be. They might be professionals, but it seemed to Alice they had not been thorough in thinking through the possible results of their recommendation. That night Alice had another lonely cry in the bathroom, finding little relief to her misery. Ralph kept company with the TV, his way of trying to keep his own suffering at bay and shield himself from Alice's pain.

# Melanie

As a preschool child, Melanie once reverentially held a baby chick in her cupped hands as some of her classmates awaited their turn. From the deep well of childhood wisdom, she cooed to it in a soft voice, "All new life is sweet, and so are you." She was a vulnerable child who responded to that quality in others in a way that was charmingly naïve. She never lost that trait as she grew to become a young adult.

After the first overwhelming experience of mental illness and some subsequent setbacks, Melanie learned to rebuild the shattered pieces of her self, to regain her innate dignity and to normalize her life. To accomplish that, she learned all she could about her illness, its cycles and manifestations. She developed the capacity to endure the misery of the disease and that of some of the therapies her doctors used to try to help her. Her own very strong survival instinct was likely the most effective weapon in her arsenal. With time and effort, she learned to identify the warnings that signaled the start of an episode, to seek hospitalization before a crisis struck, and then to bring the destructive elements of her illness under control so she could once more get on with her life. Melanie later wondered about the role her illness might have played in her parents' divorce. After a while she became satisfied that there were other more decisive factors.

PART 2

# Alice

The sky was gray as lead. It was like the predawn of an overcast day that threatened to be stormy and perhaps violently so. Alice stood alone in near darkness inside a large stone building. She stood in a corridor so shadowy that she knew only by the feel of it she was standing in ashes up to her waist. They were light and fluffy, like dry snow. She stood for a moment and then pulled herself forward once more, small swirls arising from the disturbed surface. She had no sense of time. How had she come to this place? Perhaps a repetition of such steps brought her here.

She forged ahead, making slow progress. The light inside the building increased slightly, making more of the structure visible. The ceiling soared into Gothic arches still in shadows high above her. She came to a doorway that opened into a raised cloister. The leaden sky, the stone of the building, and the ashes were all similar shades of gray. Entering the cloister, she saw it was a very large rectangle that ran around the inside walls of the building and surrounded an enormous courtyard.

The high arched openings admitted a silvery ambient light, encouraging her to move forward. Still wading through ashes, she moved to the edge of the arch, and peered through only to see the entire courtyard also filled with ashes. They lay in drifts against the side of the building opposite her. There seemed no way out. The massive building surrounded her on all sides, and the drifts of ashes looked like they might be even deeper than she was tall. She began to take stock of her situation.

What would happen if she jumped from the cloister down into the courtyard? Would she be buried in the ash? If she did jump, could she dig herself out if she had to? Could she climb back up into the cloister? There seemed to be no retreat and no advance, unless she was willing to risk the unknown. Some instinct of faith provided her the courage to move forward. The nearest ashes in the courtyard visible from where she stood looked no deeper than those she was presently wading through. If she chose to act, she might discover something that would help her. Unless she kept going, she would never know for sure. Hopefully, she pulled herself over the balustrade and dropped into the courtyard. The ashes where she now stood were ankle-deep, but there was still no sign of an exit. Was it utterly impossible to escape from this prison? Desolation seeped into her, like a heavy humid mist that rises from a pond on a cold morning and hovers above the surface like a thick blanket. Alice awoke shuddering. Outside the open window, an early morning fog muted the cries of birds and obscured everything but the ivy on the brick chimney.

***

A time comes when one finally realizes that one can be responsible only for one's own actions and behavior. Nothing works without cooperation and reciprocation. Alice finally understood that no matter what attempt she made, or would ever think to make to revive their marriage, hers would always be a one-sided endeavor. After Brad's death, she promised Ralph to give it her best effort. As time went on, she thought that maybe companionship would have to be enough to strive for. But now, without a corresponding commitment from him, she knew that nothing would ever be accomplished. That there was no reciprocation on his part spoke as unmistakably as if he himself voiced the truth that Alice heretofore chose to disbelieve: the marriage no longer interested him. Her faith in her own ability to work hard enough for there to be a resolution had sustained her effort as Alice moved through each day. Ralph was not about to disillusion her.

Alice had been pounding—no longer timidly knocking—at the door of an empty relationship that would never swing open in response to her summons, however long she persisted. She thought she importuned at the entrance to an edifice. It was only a stage set, and Ralph had long since vacated even those premises. She must accept the finality of it and take on the responsibility to make her own way out.

If the years with Ralph were devoid of marital intimacy, Alice found constructive ways to sublimate her energy in outlets that challenged her to grow. New experiences that she encountered in the world beyond the precinct of her home liberated her to feel some of the excitement and fulfillment that she so craved. Her relationship with Brad revitalized her, something that would never be possible while she remained married to Ralph.

It had been many years since their sex life died. With each of his infidelities, Ralph had given away pieces of himself to others; less and less remained of him in his relationship with his wife. Alice could no longer remember a night when his diminishing presence was not swathed in sheets and blankets as if seeking immunity from her. She finally thought to ask herself, "If I am so smart, what am I doing here?"

Their beautiful home on the harbor never mellowed Ralph. That was a failed effort. His face was turned inward and away from the abundant life teeming around him. All the daily marvels that he might have taken joy in, and that should have excited a man who enjoyed life in the out-of-doors—the changing colors of the sky, the rising and setting of the sun and moon, the lifting and flowing of the tides, the change of seasons, the birds that fished along the shoreline and called across the water, the migrating ducks beneath their windows, quacking their presence to each other on moonlit nights—in short, everything that gave Alice constant joy meant nothing to him. He rejected this ceaseless flow of blessed offerings tendered by nature's world.

Alice would forever cherish what it meant to her to live there: the terrible magnificence of storms offshore, the beauty of calm and peaceful days, and the iodine smell of algae baking in the sun at low tide mingled with the sweet fragrance of beach roses. The environment literally flowed through her home, to nourish and expand her soul. Alice continued to believe that moving there had been the best thing they could have done to revive their marriage. It just had not worked out according to her hopeful plan. She knew that the time was approaching when it might be necessary for her to part with this place that so completely held her heart.

Life teaches us to expect change. Alice had learned that usually when anything was taken away, the space would soon be filled by something new and often better than what had departed. The job she lost during the emergencies of Melanie's illness was replaced by a short-term position. That opened up new challenges, required her to develop new relationships, learn to walk the corridors of political power, and connect with others to align her interests with theirs. It would help her to advance professionally—very important when the time came to seek new employment in the aftermath of divorce.

At first, the excitement of her new job and the energy required to ascend that learning curve were enough to distract her from the deteriorating situation at home. As the weeks progressed, Alice settled into her new responsibilities. It was clear that during her commitment to this interim situation would be the best time for her to file for the divorce she knew was unavoidable. It would be a doubly difficult time for her: she would have to undergo two major life changes at the same time—divorce and another job search—and she might possibly suffer the loss of her home as well. The reward for all of that sacrifice would be a completely new beginning for the balance of her life. That, after all, was what she strove for. Halfway measures would leave her twisting in the wind. She couldn't bear to think about allowing that to happen. She was ready to begin a new life. She could do it. She had to do it.

Alice spent some time seeking references for local divorce attorneys. She chose Phoebe to represent her because she felt more comfortable telling her story to a woman. Alice wanted her pain acknowledged by someone she felt might better understand it. She believed that the more open she could be with her attorney, the better the outcome when everything ended. She was determined that would surely happen in the foreseeable future.

Phoebe did not believe in wasting time. During their initial meeting, they just barely finished introducing themselves to each other when Phoebe launched into an outline of all the milestones in the process, and the likely timeline for them to be achieved. She summed it up, "Expect that the divorce could take as long as a year to be completed, but Ralph cannot stop it from happening. He might try to delay things, but he cannot leave you hanging by simply refusing to acknowledge your petition to divorce him. We'll have a lot of work to do, but you will eventually have your freedom."

After listening to some of Alice's story, Phoebe gave her some advice: "Regardless of whether you retain me or anyone else to represent you, be sure you get yourself a good counselor. That's the most effective way to resolve any personal issues. The counselor will also provide support for you to handle problems that come up during the divorce process. I can't tell you what those might be, but I have seen it happen far too often. Too many people get overwhelmed, and become stymied when they try to go it alone.

"Given Ralph's track record, I think the divorce is likely to take at least a full year or maybe even longer, to be completed. From what you've told me, he's going to be difficult. You'll need some professional help to deal with him successfully."

In Phoebe's opinion, counseling would leave her healed—certainly enough for her to be able to move on with as clean a break as possible once everything was final. Alice would have enough to keep her occupied as the process unfolded, and then much more to do once it ended and she was free. Alice carefully considered all that Phoebe said.

A few days later, after a reprise of the dream of ashes, she committed herself to act. Alice wrote and delivered the check to engage Phoebe's services. That same day, as if she had them in the can and ready to go, Phoebe filed the divorce papers in the County Superior Court. It was done.

\*\*\*

Ironically, it was on Father's Day that she would tell Ralph of her decision. That morning, Alice came down early. The gurgling coffee pot filled the kitchen with a comforting aroma. Alice poured some of it, fresh, hot and black, into her favorite hand-thrown mug and carried it carefully through the door out onto the deck where she could watch the sun rise over the beach. As she gazed at the peaceful scene, she was content. It felt to her like the last few minutes before a performance when all the actors had learned their lines, and everyone was in their place and ready to begin. All that was needed was for the curtain to rise to reveal the setting and cue the actors to initiate dialogue and action. The appropriate moment was still a few hours distant.

Eventually, Alice went back upstairs and dressed, then busied herself in the house to wait for the "right" moment—wondering how there could ever be one. Later, when Ralph came downstairs to get his coffee and settle in to read the Sunday morning newspaper, was not the right time. Alice went out for a short walk to calm her jittery nerves. As the morning progressed and mid-day neared, there was suddenly an opportune moment. Alice told him then, quickly and honestly. She did not see how this could possibly have come as a surprise to him, and thus did not anticipate his response.

He was in shock. A series of expressions flickered across his startled face—surprise, dismay, fear, puzzlement, relief. A smile twitched the corners of his mouth and disappeared almost as soon as it became recognizable. His face returned to its initial look of startled disbelief.

"Well, that takes a load off my shoulders." He sounded relieved by her announcement. Next, a furtive look darted across his features. "You're taking your paycheck away from me." Alice was stunned and remained silent as she watched his continuing reaction. His face twitched. The corner of his mouth turned down. He removed his glasses and wiped a hand across his eyes.

A rancid taste filled Alice's mouth. She perceived the beginning of a migraine aura, the scintillations developing from somewhere far back inside her skull. Her eye muscles felt strained and her annoyance grew as her left eyelid began to twitch. Fatigue threatened to engulf her. In the next instant, all those physical symptoms gave way to a deep anger that suddenly welled up in an adrenaline rush as she reacted to how Ralph justified to himself the continuation of their marriage. What made it worthwhile for him to remain was now unmistakably clear. Apparently Ralph expected Alice to comprehend and even to agree with the good sense of his logic. The relationship conveniently served his financial purposes. Why couldn't Alice appreciate that this was a perfectly reasonable arrangement, especially for people who had survived infidelities on both sides and remained married as long as they had?

Finally, he spoke. "I don't want to talk about it. Don't tell anyone. Don't tell Melanie."

"What do you mean, 'don't tell Melanie?' Of course we have to tell her, and the rest of the family. What are you thinking?"

"Well, if we have to tell our daughter, let's do it together. Can you at least agree to that?"

"Sure, but when?"

"Let's wait a few days. I need time to think about it."

"We have to do it sooner than that. We can ask her to come and talk to us both, or we can do it separately if you are more comfortable with that. One way or another, she needs to know. The papers were filed last Friday, so it will be in the court section of the newspaper this Thursday."

Alice continued speaking to Ralph. "I've arranged to spend the week with a friend to give you some time and space to think about things. We both need that right now. We can talk more about the divorce after I come back. I asked that the papers be served to you here at home early in the morning so that you wouldn't be embarrassed or inconvenienced by the Sheriff appearing at your office."

"I don't want the divorce and I don't want to be served." He was adamant.

Alice gave him a bland look. She wasn't about to concede to him. She had deferred her action for long enough. If Ralph wanted to think he could make it all go away by ignoring it, too bad for him. He couldn't stop her. She sighed, keeping her thoughts to herself. As she opened the door to leave, Ralph came around the corner.

"Wait a minute, Alice. I just want to ask you something before you go." He looked at her with raised eyebrows. "We've been married for a long time. We've been through a lot together. When your lover died, you promised me you'd make an effort to rebuild our marriage. I made the same promise to you. What else could I have possibly done to prevent this from happening?"

Alice felt weighed down by his question. There was a whole encyclopedia's worth of things she could have called upon to frame her answer. She could have made a list a mile long if she had had the time. Instead she settled for simply saying, "You could have cared more about me, and about Melanie, and about making the marriage work."

"How do you mean that?"

She wondered why he was suddenly so attentive to details when his interest in their life together had become so superficial. That was uncharacteristic of him. Instead of trying to craft a complex response to his question, she just replied, "You could have shown us more of your face than of your back."

"Well, Alice, that same thing might just as well apply to you. Look at all the times you were away from the house."

Alice paused to reflect on the legitimacy of what Ralph had just said. He was right about her being away from the house probably most of the time—days when she was in school or working, as well as days spent on household errands. Ralph had a point, she thought, although it was not one that she agreed with. Nonetheless it seemed valid to him. She looked him in the eye and told him that. Then she said, "The difference is, I knew when to come home. I tried my best to keep my promise to you, but without your reciprocation, nothing I could do would ever be enough to make it work."

\*\*\*

Alice felt as if every day of that next week was a gift crafted especially for her. She began to feel pleased about how far she had progressed, in spite of the distance left to travel before she would be free. She had time to talk with her friends about her situation over dinner. They understood her decision and shared their own observations. She felt at times she was hearing her private thoughts expressed as if they were able to read them directly from her own mind. It comforted her and confirmed to her that she was doing the right thing. It was a week filled with grace.

She called Melanie and tried to explain her situation. Alice vowed to herself that she would not initiate a "blame game." She believed her daughter needed to have a good relationship with each parent. Alice told her that she and Ralph had grown apart from each other and were better off to end their marriage and go their separate ways. They were no longer compatible and the marriage needed to be dissolved.

"We're both good people," she told her daughter. "We just have not been good together for quite a long time."

Melanie acted as if she were surprised at the news, and disbelieving. She seemed skeptical of Alice's motives, whatever they might be, and was distant and cool when talking with her mother. Alice tried hard to explain the divorce in a way that she thought would make sense to Melanie: "It takes two committed people to make a marriage work. Ralph's attitude is that if I think something is wrong, it's my problem and none of his concern. I should just go and fix it, and then let him know when everything is back on track so he can return to the usual.

We can't talk about anything, so we cannot have an argument or confrontation, or even discussion. There's no chance to try to mend what's wrong or to make any changes. Ralph cannot stand anything that he thinks might threaten the status quo. There's simply nothing left between us. I can't trust him. I don't feel very confident that being open with him accomplishes anything. I just can't go on like that. It's become much too painful for me." Alice sincerely hoped that her daughter was equipped to understand what she so earnestly tried to communicate to her.

***

"I refuse to move out," Ralph asserted as Alice made her exit from the house. "So don't expect to come back and find me gone. No way."

As soon as she returned from her retreat, she moved her things out of the bedroom she once shared with him. For the first time he seemed to fully realize what was happening. That night whenever the sounds of his movements would begin in the adjacent room, and gradually grow loud enough to intrude upon her, she forced herself to lie quietly in her bed. She could scarcely breathe, listening to him pound the mattress and cry noisily, "No! No! No!"

It was all Alice could do to keep herself from intervening. She knew that if she did, all the effort she made to get just this far would be lost. She believed that Ralph would take it as a weakness on her part, and as evidence he could make her return to life with him on his terms. She reminded herself over and over, that night and others like it, of what she suffered from his determination to lock her outside of his life. The following morning, they passed in the doorway. Alice was returning from an early walk. Ralph was leaving for the office.

He greeted her, "We really need to talk about this."

"How about after dinner this evening; are you planning to be home?"

Ralph turned and nodded, "Perfect," without hesitating on his way out the door.

On her way to work, Alice mulled it over. By the time she parked the car and was walking toward the building that housed her office, she believed Ralph would initially try to hang on to the marriage. Alice wanted to avoid focusing on personal matters, although realistically those would be the underlying motive for the conversation. A channel of communication now had to be opened between them for the issues involved with the divorce. She expected a difficult beginning, and so she made up an agenda for them to use that evening. She itemized the issues: "House," "Boat," "Financial," and "Other Assets." She decided that should be specific enough to direct the discussion toward matters concerning the divorce, but vague enough as to not look threatening. It was adequate for a beginning.

\*\*\*

Dinner was long since ended, and it was getting late. Their discussion began in a friendly tone, but deteriorated as the evening progressed. Ralph grew angry, petulant, and seemed to cling to denial that the divorce would really happen. "I've taken a look at our joint assets. I really don't like the idea that you want to have the house. In fact, I'd be opposed to it." Ralph pushed back from the table and folded his arms across his chest.

"I could only do that if I could have the place at its assessed value. As you've pointed out many times, it isn't worth what we paid for it. You've never cared that much about the place anyway."

"No, it's worth more than we paid for it. That's what you've always insisted."

"We'll have to get a professional appraisal. That should give us the information that we don't have in our hands right now. It doesn't make sense to keep on arguing about it tonight. If we can't agree about the house, then I'll ask for all our assets to be pooled for an agreed-upon split. That would include the sale of the house, and be a perfectly reasonable request," Alice responded firmly.

He insisted to her that his company was trying to force out some of the older people. "What if they terminate my job and force me to take early retirement?"

Alice took that with grim humor. "I've got my own job situation to deal with, and it is a lot more immediate than that," she reminded him. She was determined not to let their discussion be highjacked by any of his hypothetical problems.

He threw up his hands, saying he didn't know what to do. She understood that to be a rhetorical comment. For some time, they continued to argue in that vein. It finally ended about midnight when neither of them could think of anything that had not already been said and both were completely exhausted.

\*\*\*

After several weeks of Ralph's consistent early morning disappearances, Alice became annoyed, and the gloves came off. She called Phoebe to say that trying to serve Ralph at home wasn't working because Ralph had decided that if he couldn't be served the papers, the divorce couldn't happen. Alice then asked Phoebe to arrange for Ralph to be served at work.

When the Sheriff arrived at the office with the papers, Ralph either was not there or didn't choose to acknowledge his presence. Subsequent water cooler conversations and the whispered exchanges between office staff resulted in gossip about Ralph and his unfortunate situation. There was some speculation about a possible long-ago office romance between Ralph and one of the secretaries.

\*\*\*

"Did you find a counselor?" Phoebe demanded Alice make that a much higher priority. "This will be a long legal process, and you are going to need to think about and resolve a lot of emotional issues as you go through it. It'll be easier for you if you have the right kind of help. Lawyers are not good counselors for that kind of thing. When it's over you'll want to have all your issues resolved instead of carrying that baggage forward into your new life."

Phoebe emphasized that as important as Alice's own divorce was to her, there were other cases competing with hers for court time, and for the time of the lawyers. Reluctantly, Alice surrendered her hope that her divorce could be resolved in less than a year. She would follow Phoebe's advice. Through her friends, Alice found Carrie, a psychologist with a local practice.

At Alice's first counseling session, Carrie asked, "Have you explained your reasons for this divorce to your daughter?"

"Not in any great detail. Just told her that we are both good people, but we are no longer good together." She outlined the conversation, ending, "We have gone as far as we can with each other and now before we get much older, we need to part, and continue on our separate paths."

Carrie insisted, "She needs to comprehend what life has been like for you, continuing in an unhappy marriage. She deserves to know. Otherwise she'll never have the means to understand you."

This would be a tough assignment, but after some lengthy discussion it was one which Alice agreed to undertake. She thought it was all so transparent to Melanie that she really didn't need a detailed explanation, one which would have been terribly painful for Alice to deliver. As it turned out, even a grown child who has lived with parents trapped in a loveless marriage and who has witnessed the daily disconnect, really does need to hear a justification and have the chance to question the decision.

When Alice again reached out to Melanie, she appeared once more to listen with a degree of reserve, but still gave Alice the impression she respected her feelings. Then Melanie confronted her with a question that seemed to come right out of the blue—"Don't you want your family any more?"

Alice was stunned to silence. After a few moments' pause, Melanie added, "That's what Dad told me."

Alice's eyes filled with tears. "How could he? I'm your mother. I have always loved you. That will never change as long as I live."

They each realized how deeply Ralph's duplicity had hurt them. After a few more words of mutual comfort, they hugged and the conversation turned to happier themes. Before this meeting with her daughter, Alice felt if she at least had her understanding regardless of her willingness to support what she was doing, that would have sufficed. But Carrie had been right. Alice had not taken her explanation far enough. She was not prepared for Ralph to have lied about her intentions to their daughter. Alice's faith that in time Melanie would reach a better understanding of her choice, and that she could then reestablish her daughter's trust in her, would have been misplaced. Without Alice making that renewed effort to confide in her daughter, Melanie might never have trusted her mother again.

# Ralph

I thought things finally settled down between Alice and me. I know it was rocky for a while there, but I thought we developed some kind of agreement about the way we would live. I don't get it. Maybe I'm not the brightest sometimes, but can't a guy depend on his wife to be there for him? Maybe not.

Things were going pretty well with Melanie, so I expected that we'd have some peace and quiet around here and maybe get back into spending some time on the boat again. Angela told us about Melanie's cycle and that we were coming into a good time of year for her right now. So when Alice told me she filed for a divorce, I felt like she shot me right in the back. I mean, couldn't she have at least warned me? If I'd known, I could have been a little bit ready for it. I might have even had some idea what to do, or what to say to her. Then, of all the times she could have chosen to do it, she tells me on Fathers' Day. That really knocked me for a loop. She was so controlled about it all. I wondered if she actually ran it through ahead of time, like rehearsing a wedding. She had it all planned out, right down to having her bags packed and in her car, ready to take off. She even left a full-cooked dinner in the refrigerator for me to microwave. If she had time to think about that, why couldn't she give a thought to what I would be going through after she told me?

All the rest of that day, I went around in circles. I was more worried about myself than about my daughter. She has her own life, after all. Even though I asked Alice to hold off telling her, or anyone else for that matter, I gave Melanie a quick call. She was shocked when I told her that her mother was filing for divorce. When she asked why, I told her Alice was leaving because she didn't want to have a family any more. Well, wasn't that the truth? Melanie was outraged, just like I was. Now if Alice would only do as I asked and not open her mouth to anyone else—she was not one to go around spreading stories anyway—then I could have some time before I told Penelope. She had not been friendly with Alice for the past few years since Dad died. And Bunny! Oh, man! What was I going to say to her? Bunny has been after me for a long time to ask Alice for a divorce. But I couldn't do that. I kept telling her about Melanie's problems and all of that stuff. Family loyalty, you know.

What would Melanie think if I asked her mother for a divorce? She'd never speak to me again. At least this way, Alice is the bad guy. If I asked Alice for a divorce, I would probably have to give her the house, pay alimony, and divide my pension and my retirement savings between us—50/50 if I was lucky—which would leave me in the hole. Bunny wouldn't want to have anything to do with a loser. I say that even though I don't doubt she is committed to me.

None of that made sense, so I stayed with Alice after her lover died and we had it out about making another try at keeping our family together. It was easier. People I knew thought I was being kind to her, to keep on taking care of her like I was. Maybe they were right. Why would I want to change things? All in all, I thought it did turn into a pretty stable situation. I had my home, and the family when I wanted to see them. I could be with Bunny whenever I wanted to, and Alice would keep on working, bringing home that extra bacon and keeping the home front quiet. Not bad. Some men my age would envy what I had going. I guess I just got too used to it, and it was too good to last. As long as no one else knows except Melanie and Alice and a couple of friends, I don't have too much to worry about. This gives me some time to figure out what to do.

Oh, man! What'll I say to Penelope? She'll be in orbit over this. I know she was always jealous of Alice, especially after she started working at serious jobs and could pull in some real money. Pen really started to get down on her after Alice brought home that sports car. Once I tell Pen, I'll have to tell Bunny. I can see it now—Pen hangs up with me and immediately lifts the receiver off the hook to dial, guess who? So I better tell Bunny first. I just don't know what I want to say to her. I can see it all now. None of it makes me jump with joy. Bunny will take it as if Christmas came early and Alice just handed her the biggest gift in the whole world. Egad, Alice, what was so bad that you had to go and do this?

Wait a minute—if I don't move out of the house, it'll look like I'm trying my best to win back my wife who is breaking my heart because I'm still in love with her after all these years. That'll keep Bunny off balance long enough to give me some space while I decide how to handle things. Besides, why should I leave? I'm just as entitled to live here as she is. I'm the one who's paying for the place. Alice is the one who should move out, not me. She's the one who wants her freedom. Let her go and earn it for herself. I'd like to see her do that. She'll get nothing from me. Then she'll be sorry she ever started this divorce thing.

He went on for several hours that way. Ralph finally ate the dinner Alice left for him; he flicked on the TV some time around 11 p.m. to catch the late news, and fell asleep in his chair before the first item was fully reported.

*** 

The next morning was Monday, the beginning of a new work week. Ralph vaulted out of bed as soon as the first rays of the sun entered the window, quickly showered, dressed, and left home at about 5:30 a.m., much earlier than usual. No sheriff was in sight, much less at the door. He breakfasted at Mac-

Donald's on his way to the office. Once he had eaten and was a bit less agitated, he admired the clarity of the morning air and the cloudless blue skies that beckoned him forth to begin a week of life as a bachelor.

He drove to the office, negotiating the growing stream of commuting traffic. Arriving so early that there was only one other person at their desk, he spent the morning finishing up some paperwork and making phone calls. By noon he was ready to call it a day.

Alice's announcement must have hit him harder than he thought. He decided to spend the afternoon on the boat. Even if he stayed in his slip at the marina and just did some work on the vessel, it would give him space to think. Besides, he could see the house from the boat slip. He didn't really expect Alice to show up there during the day, but if she did, he'd know it. He picked up some lunch and a six-pack of beer on his way to the boat, and then spent the rest of the day working on it with only the briefest of thoughts about his situation. Soon it was twilight. No lights came on at home. By the time he finished picking up his tools and stowing all the things he had taken out of the hatches during the afternoon—dock lines and cockpit cushions he'd spread out to dry in the sun—it was nearly dark. The dock lights illuminated his steps as he made his way land-ward. He stopped at the bar in the marina for a drink. Why not?

Ralph hated to come home to a dark house. It may have been something buried deep in his subconscious mind because it was so unvarying. He was aware of it, but not in the way of acknowledging it as anything especially important. It was just something peripheral to him. If brought to his attention, he lightly tossed it off. Alice found it irritating. She wondered on the rare occasions when she came home later than Ralph, why he could not just go inside, turn on the lights and start dinner. When she did come home to a dark empty house, it would seem to be no more than five minutes before he showed up. She always wondered how many times he circled the block, waiting.

Alice's declaration now gave Ralph a multitude of issues to

resolve. Entering the darkened dwelling, he felt plagued by the residue of everything that happened the previous afternoon, starting with his first reaction of disbelief that she really meant it and would go through with it. How could she? What was she trying to prove? Then he considered the financial implications, beginning with the loss of her monetary contributions to the household, to filing a joint tax return versus filing as an individual, to the health insurance she carried through her employer that covered them both. How was he going to make up all of that? He was worried about the money. He always filed their tax returns late. He enjoyed teasing Alice when she would be annoyed about that and ask him why he would even think about doing that when the IRS owed them a refund. "Why on earth do you think you need a postponement?" would be her irritated demand.

His muttered response would begin with something that sounded to her like, "Just because…." quickly sliding off to unintelligible nothingness. This year, unless he could get away with demanding they file a joint return, it might mean he would have a real reason to postpone. He sighed as he turned on the lights. He could see that his life was going to get a lot more complicated than it had been in a long time. The week was not productive for him, except to remind him of all the responsibilities that now started poking up like a tribe of weeds invading an orderly garden. He could not wait for Alice to come back, even if he didn't hear the words he wanted her to say to him.

# Alice

The time to begin preparing for the negotiations that would occur prior to a court date still lay ahead. The turmoil that attended the completion of her filing was now ended. For the moment, Alice felt as if sheltered in an unexpected refuge. She was relieved to have gotten this far without some intervening crisis. She had worked hard to complete the first part of the process, and now had to face specific issues. She and Phoebe had to agree on an in-depth strategy to deal with those; then Alice would have her next "to-do" list. The chance to relax a bit felt welcome, however soon it would end.

Over the days that followed, Alice began to experience a growing sense of well-being. As hope and the promise of freedom waxed, she began to feel lighter and less encumbered. Still, she knew it wasn't over yet. A lot of work remained to be done—by herself, with Phoebe, with Ralph and whoever his attorney might be—but the end was now becoming more of a reality to her than the mere hope it had been at the outset. Alice began to be lifted by the perceived approach of her freedom. As yet there was no counterweight of renewed demands on her, so the energy of her anticipation and excitement grew until it reached euphoric levels. If this were a race, and she could have sprinted to the finish line, she would have.

*** 

One evening a few weeks after the filing, Alice picked up the phone to be greeted by a familiar, rich, vibrant male voice. It was one she had not heard for many years and that she instantly remembered but never expected to hear again. A low snigger followed by a click, alerted Alice that in another part of the house, Ralph also picked up the receiver and listened to the greeting before hanging up. "Well, let him think what he wants," was Alice's serene thought as she acknowledged the caller by name.

Eric was a good friend to Alice throughout their college years. They were such close confidants then that everyone expected he and Alice would end up together. But Eric never declared himself in that way to Alice, and she did not to him—in those days women didn't do such things. Then Alice became involved with Ralph and Eric stepped aside. Soon after Alice married Ralph, Eric altogether disappeared from her life. He moved to the West Coast, and from time to time, Alice heard a snippet here and a comment there. Filling in the blanks she had long since deduced that he was happy and fulfilled.

"It can't be you, Eric. After all these years! Has someone died?" was her puzzled greeting. Their circle of college friends had been small, and most of them went out to the West Coast after graduation. Alice and only a few others remained in New England.

"I looked in the Alumni Directory to see if you were listed. I'm glad you were. No one has died, at least that I know of. Still looking for the silver lining, aren't you?" He chuckled.

After a few brief salutatory comments, it was as if their last conversation occurred no more than a week ago. They simply picked up where they had left off, and spoke at some length. Alice finally asked what prompted his call. Eric told her that he would be coming east the following week, on business. "I've been very nervous about just calling you out of the blue like this, but I decided that this trip is the excuse I needed to do that."

Eric spent some years after he first landed in California

teaching art history in a private school. His interest in the area's museums and its artist colonies brought him many new friendships, which in turn led to him working with a partner to start one gallery, then another, and finally led to the idea of starting another new venture, this time back East.

The first gallery in San Francisco became very successful. It took a long period of trial and effort to get it going. He spent a whole decade of his life focused on that. Once its popularity began to take off, the next gallery, opened in Honolulu, totally consumed him. Now he was to meet with some colleagues in Boston to discuss a joint venture there. This would be his first trip back to the northeast since he left after college graduation. Over the years he thought of their friendship and every so often found that he missed the days when he could talk to her about anything, anytime. As the conversation began to wind down, Eric asked if she would be able to meet him for lunch while he was in town. Alice never hesitated in her reply. She couldn't wait to see him again. That night, she dreamed that she and Eric were together as they had been in college. The dream left her feeling radiant and next morning as she left for work, she knew she carried the glow of a well-loved woman.

***

Eric's unexpected call took Alice completely by surprise. Their meeting soon followed. She could never have imagined it happening at all, never mind that it happened the way it did. Alice met Eric at a restaurant near the State House where she had some appointments scheduled with various legislators and their staffs. They immediately recognized each other in spite of the intervening years, which had left her with some earned wrinkles and him with a receding hairline. They embraced like long-lost lovers. A single red rose—if one had been placed on their table—would have been appropriately poignant. Alice had less than two hours and Eric not even that before they were ob-ligated to return to their respective business engagements.

After Eric told her about his plans for the new gallery and the reception he'd received that morning from some potential backers, the conversation took a personal turn. Alice outlined her situation to him, telling Eric she didn't know what the future held for her once the divorce was completed. She was willing to do whatever she must to restart her life in a positive direction. She talked a little about Melanie. When she finished, she asked Eric if he had ever married and did he have children? He seemed surprised by her question.

"Alice," he began tentatively, "all that time we were friends in college, did you never realize that I am gay? Didn't Ralph ever say anything to you? He was aware of it. I was sure he must have said something to you about it."

"Never," was Alice's stunned response. "Of course I didn't. It never entered my mind. Who ever thought about things like that back then, especially anybody in our crowd?" For once, she was at a loss for words. Her mouth hung open as she stared as if seeing him clearly for the first time—the crisp line of his jaw that summed up his fit physique, the intelligent gray eyes that studied her closely in return.

Eric intently watched her expression change as he continued, "I thought you already knew that about me."

She was stunned by his revelation. She never suspected it. Their friendship, the whole thing that blossomed between her and Eric, and Eric's departure from her once she was involved with Ralph, fell into place. Until this very moment she had never realized that her relationship with Ralph had taken such an enormous toll on her friendship with Eric. Years ago she was disappointed that he did not at least say something to her at the time when her relationship with Ralph began. Now it was completely understandable. Worse, Ralph had known something about Eric that she did not. She recalled his derisive chuckle when she picked up the phone and heard Eric's voice. Well, so what? She was thrilled just to be back in touch with him. His friendship still meant the world to her. Now it was based on who they truly were. That was what really mattered. All at once, Alice asked him, "Who do you see when you look at me?"

"I see my friend Alice, who is still the same energetic,

well-meaning, bright and beautiful woman as always," was his considered response. "Why do you ask?"

"I still think of us as who we once were, when we were back in college. It was a magical time; life as we would choose to make it was still ahead of us. I think about how young and naïve I was then. Very little has turned out as I recall imagining it. I really can't blame Ralph for diverting me from following my dream. I was certainly willing to follow him instead. But I have missed you, Eric. I took your friendship for granted, and depended on it. I guess I made one choice that turned out right."

\*\*\*

Following their luncheon, Alice's head filled with thoughts about Eric's sudden re-appearance in her life, his unexpected admission to her, how she reacted to him, and he to her, and how they left things when they parted ways again. She wanted to talk this over with Carrie.

In every divorce that Alice witnessed among her friends, a man who had not been visible or present before the partners separated soon entered the picture. He might be a business or social acquaintance of the husband, or a neighbor, or someone from the office, but his entrance always included an introduction that gave him automatic credibility. She was amazed at how many such stories she had heard over the years, whether directly, or repeated to her at second-hand.

Alice's friend Rosalyn once shared her story of being divorced by a husband involved with another woman. Ros met such a man and was very excited that not long after her husband's announcement, someone else began to court her. It took away the sting from the humiliation she felt. Ros shone like a new diamond and was easily drawn into an affair. The euphoria, the radiance of feeling desirable and loved, and Ros' self esteem were all destroyed when the affair abruptly ended. She was left far more vulnerable than before, as the loss of both husband and lover now doubled the score of what she saw as her failed relationships with men. It was a very destructive experience, exacting greater punishment than the divorce itself. Ros felt labeled a failure. She was emotionally confused and off-balance.

Whatever else he did, her former husband never let on that he knew of the affair and that saved her from even greater distress. Ros tried her best to bear a heavy burden and she stumbled. No one offered to come to her rescue. In truth, no one could. Just as with anyone in such a situation, her rescue was her own responsibility.

To get past the whole sorry situation, Ros steeled herself to look squarely and honestly at the character of the man who made her a victim to his destructive game and at why she was so eager to be complicit. She treated this examination as if it were a mirror held up for her to see herself as he had and show her what made her susceptible to his advances. Ros recognized her vulnerability and gave it credence. She acknowledged the injustice, felt the pain and expressed her anger. Ros then set it aside and concentrated on making the best possible end to her divorce.

Carrie began to smile as Alice then told the story of her friend Eric, and by the end, she was laughing. "And what do you make of Eric? Didn't he enter the scene for you with about the same timing as the man in the story about Ros? Is he really gay?"

Alice stopped to think for a moment. "We already had a trusting relationship right back to our college days, but I never knew that about him."

Carrie prompted her. "Maybe that's why Ralph never hinted to you what he knew about Eric. It could have made you so angry you might have handed him his walking papers. He was afraid to take that chance. Besides, he knew you wouldn't be able to leave him for Eric. Best of all, you didn't even suspect it."

Alice sat there as if in a trance. A few moments passed before she spoke. "These are two distinctly different experiences. Ros encountered a predator. I reconnected with a trusted friend, and there's no chance that could ever turn into an affair. The common thread is that he appeared at the exact moment when most needed, as if on cue."

Carrie offered a thought: "There always seems to be a facilitator who enters early on and acts to further distance the divorcing man or woman from their partner. I'm using the word "facilitator" because it implies two things—first, it has the sense of easing something along, and then it also implies duplicity. You may meet someone else who shows up out of the blue and have a very different experience."

***

Days turned to weeks, and the weeks slowly accumulated into months. Alice diligently filled out the paperwork Phoebe sent her along with updates that seemed to always be that there was no court date yet on the horizon, and it would take a while to get her case on the docket. Alice continued to plug away at her list of tasks.

Ralph went on living in the house with Alice, coming home most evenings for dinner. There was a semblance of life as it had been lived before the filing, but now, with the knowledge that there would be an end, it felt more stiff and constricted. Ralph's behavior was a curious mix of correctness and courtliness, which was most unusual for him. When she spoke, he attended. He willingly contributed to discussion about most topics. Occasionally, he even ventured to discuss some minor points about the divorce with her. Ralph did not especially feel the need to let Alice know of his plans, but he became suddenly considerate about telling her when he would not be there until later in the evening.

"How could you stand that?" Carrie asked Alice when she learned that in addition to Ralph continuing to live in the house with her, she still made dinner for him every evening. Mechanically, Alice would put out a dinner on the counter, wrapped in plastic and ready for the microwave should Ralph show up at all and want to eat before turning in for the night. Often she disposed of an uneaten meal the next morning. While admitting her discomfort at the arrangement, Alice's constant reply was that she was accustomed to doing it. It was something of a ritual. Once in a while when they ate together, she thought they even had meaningful and helpful conversation.

\*\*\*

Each morning when Alice looked out the windows, she loved everything she saw. She had so firmly believed that moving into this beautiful place would help to soften Ralph and encourage him romantically, and could barely countenance the reality that it hadn't helped in the least. When Alice entered and firmly closed the door of her own bedroom at night, she was relieved that Ralph was gone from the private part of her day. It felt to her a small but important indicator of progress in the right direction.

Alice reached out to her friends for comfort, as she told each of her decision to file for divorce. Their responses ranged from surprise to sympathy. A couple of women even told her they too thought about doing the same thing. Alice encouraged them not to use her state of affairs as an example for their own situations. Not all things belong in all lives. After a while, Alice decided this was the way some of her friends could most meaningfully express their support.

During the months of working at their jobs and coming home to a place now lacking the last vestiges of being a home, Alice assumed a pattern of treating Ralph almost as she would a brother. Sometimes she thought he seemed a bit overwhelmed by it all. At times, she felt that was true of herself as well.

\*\*\*

One evening, Alice asked Ralph whether he had found a lawyer. "No. I haven't had time. Maybe yours could handle both of us."

A quick call to Phoebe the next day put that idea to rest. "It's a conflict of interest. You really wouldn't want me to do that anyway. Tell him he needs to get his own counsel."

Alice explained to Ralph that Phoebe could not work for

them both, and that to protect his interests, he'd better find an attorney, as the divorce would happen whether he wanted it to or not. She shared with him the other names she received as recommendations in response to her search for "tough but fair" legal representation, and let him know she had not approached any of them. She thought that as he had asked how she found Phoebe, he could use the remainder of her brief list as a place to start. He declined, telling her he was not interested.

# Ralph

What did Alice think I would do anyway, with that list of lawyers she gave me? Was I supposed to go to one of her friends and ask for help? I don't think so. I consulted with my friends down at the dock. I told them I was looking for someone with a reputation for being really tough, and who would give her what she deserves. I didn't especially care about the "fair" part. She was the one who declared war on me. She was the one who started all this. She thought she was going to leave me behind in the dust. I thought that if I could share the lawyer with her, I could save myself some money and also slow things down, at least long enough for me to get my feet back under me. Then I could just tap the brakes every once in a while, when I felt like doing it. I'd probably frustrate the lawyer and get her to quit the case. Then where would Alice be? Nowhere. But that didn't work out.

If that wasn't enough to worry about, there was Bunny. She couldn't have been happier. She had been after me for a long time to divorce Alice, and now Alice was divorcing me. Bunny was going to get what she wanted without lifting a finger. If Bunny had any problem at all, it would be trying to decide what to complain about now that everything was going her way. To keep all of Bunny's issues on the back burner, I agreed to buy a place that was under construction and have it finished for her—now us. I hadn't quite decided how I wanted to handle that. If I bought the property and rented it to Bunny, then she'd have a place to live where we could be together, but she would have to be able to pay the mortgage expenses, at least until after the divorce. If I took out a mortgage, that would show up on my credit report. What if that was something the lawyers looked at for the divorce? I'd be in a real pickle. I'm not sure I could even qualify for a mortgage on top of Alice's house and the boat. It looked like, to pay for the place outright, I would have to take the cash out of the funds I saved from bonuses that over time I had hidden away from Alice. That would be harder for Alice's lawyer to find out about unless she was going to search for stuff like that. I didn't expect Phoebe to do that. But, whenever Bunny moved in, unless she was paying me rent, I'd never be able to get her out of there if we broke up for some reason. She's going to expect that we would live together once the place was finished, or why would I spend my money on it? She'd be right about that. Just a thought—whoa! Do I have to put the place in her name to keep it hidden until the divorce is all over? That'd be taking a chance. What if we broke up and I wanted to get the title back afterward?

I doubt if I could have filed for a divorce that would force Alice out of our home so it could be sold. One thing about Alice making the first move—without a kid under 18 living at home, I'm not obliged to let her have the house. Economically it makes sense for me to stay put until the divorce is all over, and keep on telling her I can't afford to live anywhere else. She can't argue about it too much because she knows she can't pay the mortgage on her own. My new place is still under construction. That'll take a while to complete and get an occupancy permit. Until then, I can't be homeless. Why should I be, when I can just stay where I am? I only need to hang on with Alice until the new house is finished. Then I can make my move. So I have to make sure this divorce takes a long enough time so I have a seamless transition, as they say. That solves that.

After I checked with my friends about attorneys, I decided it would be easier to pick someone local from the Yellow Pages. There was a name there that some of them mentioned to me, so I called the guy and laid out my situation with Alice. He agreed to meet and talk about representing me, so now she had her lawyer and I nearly had mine. A couple of guys should be able to win out over a couple of girls any day. I felt confident.

\*\*\*

What really impressed me about Hubert was the man's sense of outrage about my situation and the energetic way he expressed that to me. Here was a man who really understood me, who believed in my rights and wanted to rectify the wrong that Alice was trying to inflict on me. I thought Hubert was a bit strong on the punishment angle, but that might be okay given the sharp broad that Alice was. Maybe Hubert had been downed by a woman in his past, and this looked like a way to get some back. I detected that he had a strong sense of pride. I thought he might be a little overbearing about some things, but that would be okay. It's easier to back down a bit than to recover from not being aggressive enough at the outset. As I left his office, I recalled one of the guys saying that the best lawyer for me would be one who would treat my situation as if he were pushing his own agenda. That seemed reasonable to me. Maybe those were the vibes I'd gotten from Hubert. If so, that was just fine.

Hubert picked up on the mention of the phone call that Alice received from Eric, and asked if I thought Alice might be having an affair. I thought about it, but once I learned it was Eric on the phone, and that he lived on the West Coast, it didn't add up. And I didn't see any reason to revive the past, so I didn't tell Hubert the tale of Alice's dead lover.

Alice didn't know about Bunny, so I sure didn't want to take the chance that if Hubert went after Alice, she'd find out and turn the tables on us. I'd have too much to lose if that happened. So, I made a clean breast of my relationship with Bunny. Hubert agreed it would be best to leave that subject alone.

We talked about household goods. I thought that since all the stuff I really cared about had come from my family, I'd expect

Alice wouldn't want any of it. Hubert suggested I ask Alice to list everything in the house and divide it up between her and me so we could discuss who wanted what. That seemed like a good idea; she'd probably think I was trying to be a good guy about something. It might earn me a point or two.

That brought everything down to what the financial settlement would look like, and whether Alice knew anything about the money I had kept concealed from her. I hated to mention anything about that to Hubert, but I had a problem and needed his help. He had to be ready to defend me if she ever got to open up that can of worms. We talked seriously about all of it for a long time. He advised me to be careful about how I filled out the disclosure form. "When you get it all finished, we'll go over it with a fine tooth comb to make sure you're in good shape. Meanwhile, get me the name and address of her lawyer. I'll take care of her."

Being so concerned about the big money questions, I never even thought to watch the clock and keep track of his time. When I finally left Hubert's office, I felt reassured about having someone on my side, for a change, who knew the ropes.

***

The next evening, I met Bunny for dinner. Afterward, we went back to her place to talk about my situation. I told her about meeting Hubert and how confident I felt in using him for the divorce proceedings. Meanwhile, I'd stay in the house with Alice and make an effort to get along with her to see if I could keep her in the dark about Bunny.

"I don't like it," was Bunny's response to that ploy. "It makes me nervous. What if she decides she doesn't want to go through with it because you are suddenly being so nice to her? Then what will you do? All she has to do is tell your daughter that she wants a reconciliation and it'll be all over." Bunny grimaced. "Then what happens when our house is ready to move into?"

"Alice takes a long time to decide what she wants to do, but once she makes up her mind, she moves like a freight train straight down the tracks. We don't want to bring her to a stop; we just want to slow her down a little so we don't get caught short. Besides, I have big money invested in our house, more than I have in Alice's. So, you got me by the wallet as well." I thought that would make Bunny feel better. It didn't do a thing for me.

We talked a while longer; I avoided the topic of having to fill out a financial disclosure. The less Bunny knew about that, the better. I already had the upper hand with her, since my money was paying for our house. I knew Bunny wouldn't do anything to upset me, especially if it had to do with Alice. She'd stay out of sight and keep her mouth shut. In fact, at just the moment that thought occurred to me, Bunny was actually loosening my tie and unbuttoning my shirt. I loved it when she did that. I knew that meant I was going to have a very nice night.

\*\*\*

The next morning, I saw Alice as she was leaving for work. I told her I had hired a lawyer and wanted to put him in touch with Phoebe. Alice set her briefcase down long enough to pull out one of Phoebe's business cards for me to give Hubert. Then, since I got what I wanted when I asked the first question, I thought I'd try something else, so I asked if Phoebe gave her any forms to fill out. Alice responded that she had. She was working on them to prepare for a meeting that would include both of us and our attorneys. Since she told me that much, I thought I'd go for the point. "Do you have anything finished that I can look at, you know, as a model I could use to fill out my papers?"

I almost laughed when Alice refused this request and hurried out the door. I could always find a way to upset her—there was always a chink in her armor. I never had to spend a lot of time prodding to find the weak spot.

After Alice left, I went upstairs, took my time showering and then dressed for work. I picked up my towel from the bathroom floor and hung it on a rack. The last time I showered like this, I left the bathroom to answer the phone and forgot about the mess of wet towels lying in the middle of the floor. That night, when I came home I found them piled up dead center on my bed. I had been angry but didn't want to confront Alice about it, so I threw the towels in the laundry and then went to spend the night at Bunny's. Although Alice's bedroom door was closed, I knew she was in there, awake and tuned in to my reaction. I just plain refused to give her the satisfaction of yelling at her. What good would that have done anyway? Besides, it was a free pass for me to be gone again all night. But I really didn't need one.

*\*\*\**

          \*\*\*

"What am I supposed to do with this?" I asked Hubert when we sat down again to discuss the financial disclosure form. I continued to worry that if Alice ever found out how much money I had hidden away, she'd be sure to make a grab for it. We jointly owned a house and a boat, both mortgaged. Those were known assets—obviously, easy to disclose. There were no joint bank accounts. We each had retirement savings from our respective jobs.

My big concern was that if I was forced to admit to owning hidden assets, then the house I was building with Bunny would be discovered and become a huge issue. Alice might suspect I was having an affair, but so far she hadn't let on that she knew anything for sure. If she did find out, it could get really bad for me. Letting her find out about that house was in the same league as committing suicide. Not my style. I asked Hubert could I take the Fifth on that one. A fifth of what, he wanted to know, and then he just laughed. It was a deep belly laugh, like he was really entertained by all this goofy stuff. I couldn't be the first client he ever had to have problems like this. If I was, I needed a better lawyer than him to bail me out.

The other thing I had that Alice didn't know about was a cemetery plot that I had bought because it was available in a nice part of the town where I grew up and lived my whole life until she and I got married. It probably sounds dumb to rhapsodize about what a beautiful view of a small pond there is when you stand on the plot, but there it is. Someday we're all going to need someplace to go. This cemetery is well cared for, and just beautifully landscaped. Maybe the grandkids—if I ever had any—would even drop by to visit me once in a while. So here I was with an asset I could admit to having, and one that I couldn't. To give him credit, Hubert was able to control himself. His face never changed while I meandered through my thoughts.

When I finally stopped talking, he pulled himself back together and said, "You should tell her about the cemetery plot. It's big enough for the whole family, so it can be made to look like you acted responsibly when you decided to buy it. Get the rest of your family to sign consent forms to be buried there. That should be simple enough to do. They probably haven't given one thought to that, so it should be easy for you to solve this problem they don't even know they have. That'd give your purchase legitimacy—make it look like you really did do it for your family. Then tell Alice there's space for her as well and give her the forms to sign. That'll make her a co-owner. That can help a bit with your financial settlement. She'll get part of that asset and less of something else. Whatever else you may accomplish, I guarantee this will distract her from the other stuff."

I hadn't thought of it that way, but it did have the kind of logic I found appealing. After I left Hubert's office, I thought about it a whole lot more, and the idea just seemed better and better.

That night when I met Bunny for a drink after work, I talked with her about the plot and Hubert's brilliant idea. When I asked her if she'd sign on to the deal, Bunny just laughed and told me she wasn't ready yet to make any commitments about the afterlife to anyone, and she still wasn't sure about this life. Bunny just couldn't believe that Alice would have anything to do with it, never mind anyone else. She joked around a little, reciting some of her usual repertoire of Irish wake and funeral jokes. Then she said, "This material is good enough to keep people laughing about your good deed for a long time to come. You think anyone will take it seriously when you lay out your plan to them?"

That was such an obvious pun it made me wince. She was no help at all. She didn't even try to be. I bolted down the rest of my drink and said good night to her.

\*\*\*

When I finally got home, Alice was waiting for me. I wondered if she had ESP. Then she unloaded on me. "Did you think you could sell the boat without telling me?"

Holy mackerel! Hadn't I told her I had listed it for sale with the brokerage at the marina? I mean, they're right there, and they have the keys. They could show it any time they had someone who wanted to see it. She already knew about that. So what was the big deal? They had a buyer who made a reasonable offer and I had agreed to it. I thought she'd be happy when I got around to telling her about it.

"Ralph," Alice said impatiently, "You can't sell it without my signature. Were you going to have someone else sign my name? That's forgery. That boat is a jointly owned asset. The buyer cannot take title to it unless we both sign the papers. You needed to tell me you had a buyer. I'm glad. You needed to ask me to sign the Purchase and Sale Agreement. That's all. It shouldn't be a big deal. I asked Phoebe to make sure the broker understands the situation."

"I was going to tell you about it." That sounded lame, even to me. "I wasn't trying to hide anything from you. How could I?"

"Right." She turned her back to me and walked out of the room.

When I went into the kitchen I found the dinner she left for me on the counter. She couldn't have been all that angry if she did that. She didn't throw it at me. A good sign. I would have liked more of those.

\*\*\*

The next evening I came home at dinnertime thinking I'd surprise Alice, but once again she seemed to be waiting for me. I was nervous, but she had only been at work on my suggestion that she list and divide our household goods. Two copies were ready for us to discuss after dinner. I could use a session of softball before we got around to the hardball.

As I expected, everything that came from my family was on my list. There were a couple of things she had liked that I was willing for her to have. We spent a couple of hours going back and forth over the list, exchanging some items. Much to my surprise we ended up with a pretty well-balanced division that we each found we could agree to. The big item—the money—was going to be a lot harder. That was going to take more than a couple of hours. I mentioned the value of the house to her. She had definitely given that some thought. It sounded like she might have thought of only that and nothing else. Real estate values decreased since we bought the house. When I tossed out the amount we paid for the place, she responded, "That's funny. Ever since we bought this house, you've spent all the time we've lived here moaning about how it isn't worth what we paid for it. Now when the market has dropped, suddenly it is worth that much. Give me a break." Well, that convinced me I had to go to a realtor—Hubert would know which one—and get a letter of opinion as to the value of the house. At least I knew where Alice would be coming from on this one, and we would be ready for her.

*** 

A couple of days later, I went back to Hubert's office to finalize my financial statement and the list of items I planned to keep. It was still about a week before we were supposed to meet with Alice and Phoebe, so I felt I could take a breather. I decided to take a short trip to Aruba with Bunny. I needed some getaway time to relax. I bought the airplane tickets on the way home.

When Alice came in, I told her I'd been invited to go down south for a few days with some friends I had met on the dock at the marina. They were planning to do some deep-sea fishing and then head back up here. "I'd like to go even though that would mean you'd be here all alone for most of the week. You could come with me if you could get a few days off from work." Putting it to her that way, it would have floored me if she had wanted to go. I knew she'd like the time alone, she hated deep sea fishing, and besides that, she didn't have much vacation time accrued from this job. I felt I was on pretty safe ground. And, if she took it that I was trying to be nice to her, so much the better.

Alice asked me why I thought I needed permission from her to go anywhere. Regardless, she couldn't get the time off from work and it didn't appeal to her anyway. She also had to work on her financial statement and touch base with Phoebe to get ready for our big meeting the following week. Then, she wanted to take stuff out of the attic and the closets and finish boxing up what was hers and what was mine. We had a smaller attic that was in a dead space between two of the rooms on the second floor, and a larger attic above the ceilings. Alice had trouble getting into that one, so she kept everything she could in the smaller space.

I noticed that when she started separating stuff, she put my rifle and boxes of cartridges way in the back of the smaller attic. I decided to remove them before she got the bright idea of taking them to the police station to turn them in, or something ridiculous like that. So, very carefully, making it look like nothing had been disturbed, I did that and moved them into the attic above the second floor ceiling, where she wouldn't find them. Where else could I take a rifle and boxes of cartridges to hide them? Bunny wouldn't let me store them at her place. I already asked her.

I was happy to be off the hook about the trip to Aruba. No issue with my going out of state, but Hubert said that if I didn't tell Alice about the trip, she could claim I had abandoned her. That would put the divorce into legal high gear, and would sure complicate things way too much. As it was, I thought I did a pretty slick job of telling her in a way that she bought into it— and it ended up with me and Bunny taking a vacation and lying around on the beach for a week.

# Alice

Alice kept in touch with Bruce, her academic advisor during her student years at his college. When she first met him, he had been there for a while and was feeling jaded by what he must have seen as an endless sea of youngsters. A father himself, he observed the throes of later adolescence on the job, and again at home. When Alice entered the scene, as a mature woman she was a welcome relief and added some spice to those days when he saw her. She enjoyed that time of her life enormously. Bruce encouraged her to go on to graduate school. Some years later, when Melanie reached an impasse about a career decision, Alice referred her to Bruce for advice. He was highly complimented that Alice sent her daughter to him for guidance, and never forgot her trust and confidence in him.

He missed Alice, and began to invite her back to the college, sometimes as a guest lecturer, and other times to join him and his students in something special that he knew she would enjoy. Bruce understood what becoming a biologist meant to her. He observed her enthusiasm for lab work. He watched her research topics of special interest, and grow in knowledge and understanding. Alice was old enough to be a mother to most of the other students; her life experiences made her an interesting conversational partner for various members of the faculty who befriended her.

After Alice filed for her divorce, Bruce, upon hearing the news, invited her to join him and his students on the college's research vessel to trawl for specimens. "Would you like a chance to relive your carefree student days? You probably could use a break. How about spending a couple of hours at sea, away from all the heavy lifting?"

Alice had loved her first such adventure and was delighted to accept. It would be like making a journey to revisit her roots.

The vessel's captain could have been the face on a seafood ad. A jaunty Greek captain's cap sat atop a full head of iron gray curly hair that reached down the sides of his face to join a beard that covered his chin. A gold earring in his pierced left ear completed the look of the dashing seaman. Captain Dawson commanded the vessel, a small shoal-draft trawler equipped with a large net that was let out to fish for specimens and then winched in to spill its contents onto the deck. Wooden doors descended into the water with the net, to hold it open during the trawl.

A day on the research vessel was a day in heaven, so far as Alice was concerned. This one was blue perfection. As the boat pulled away from the dock and headed out the channel, Alice looked back at the sun pennies sparkling in the wavelets tossing about in the vessel's wake. Absorbed in trying to identify some of the landmarks quickly receding as the vessel thrust forward, she noted the range markers coming into alignment as the captain steered for the main navigation channel. Turning toward the wheelhouse, she saw his hawklike profile as he turned to locate the buoys that marked the edge of the channel and now floated immediately ahead of them. He turned briefly, seemed to give Alice a quick wave of the hand, and then once more faced forward to monitor the boat's progress.

A few minutes later, Bruce appeared with two cups of coffee, balancing carefully as he crossed the deck toward her. "Cap'n's compliments," he shouted as he handed her one of the mugs.

She smiled at him and waved an arm to include the glorious

panorama of sky, sea and shore opening before them. "Glorious isn't it?" she yelled, just barely audible above the engine noise.

The vessel continued to steam ahead until they were clear of the harbor and inshore boat traffic. Captain Dawson handed the wheel to his mate and joined Bruce and Alice on deck. "I'd say we should be a couple of miles further out before we set the net," he advised Bruce.

"That's fine with me. That gives the mate a chance to acquaint the students with the working of the net," Bruce concurred. "Let them know how they can help setting and hauling so they can get the full experience. Lots of strong backs here; let's put 'em to work."

Smiling, the captain returned to the wheelhouse to resume control of the vessel. When the mate came on deck, the students grouped around him to hear his instructions.

After some time, Captain Dawson reduced speed and began to turn the vessel in a wide circle. Alice went to the wheelhouse and watched the sonar screen with him. He was looking for a school of fish before giving the order to set the net. After a quarter hour of looking at a mostly blank screen, a small cloud appeared to float across it. "I think this is as good a place as any," the captain remarked. When he further reduced speed, the mate came to the wheelhouse window and gave a "thumb's up" signal that they were ready to lower the net. The boat slowed down even more.

"Heave now!" the mate cried out. They all joined in to set the net out into the water behind the trawler. As the doors dropped into the water to hold the net open, the captain accelerated the engine. Even at full power, the vessel moved very slowly against the drag of the net and the doors. Now they were trawling. They would continue on this course for the entire time the net was down.

The students headed for the galley to make another urn of coffee as they prepared to wait for the trawl to be finished. The captain and mate were both in the wheelhouse, one keeping the boat on a straight course, the other consulting the sonar screen.

Bruce brought them coffee and then returned to the deck to converse with Alice and a few students who came outside to join them.

The mate left the wheelhouse long enough to confirm to Bruce that they would be on this course for another half hour. "After that," the mate said, "the captain will give the order to bring up the net to see what we have."

"Okay, ladies and gents," Bruce said to the students, "prepare to help haul out the net when we get the signal." Turning to Alice, he asked, "How are you doing?"

"I'm great. What a wonderful day. I'm so glad you invited me out here. I feel so free and so clean—just us and the sea, no other complications. Thank you for this, Bruce. I still love this stuff as much as ever."

He grinned at her. He stood there enjoying her company and soaking up the sun. Soon he called out, "There's the signal. Now we get to see what Father Neptune has sent us."

The winch groaned at first, but then turned more easily as the doors emerged from the water with a smacking sound and swung about on their chains. The mate grabbed the lines to secure them and prevent their hitting the net as it came up. Finally the net appeared and was winched in above the transom of the vessel. It was not a large catch. The students worked alongside the mate, then crowded together in anticipation. When they opened the net, the aquatic treasures spilled out onto the deck in a slippery, silver heap. Flounder, small lobsters, squid, and small finfish of local species—sea robins, stripers, drumfish, and rock bass. Whenever an offshore storm pushed the Gulf Stream closer inshore, there would even be small tropical fish in the catch. Their iridescent scales made them stand out from the darker colored local species like large shiny coins. Along with the fish, there were some glutinous strands of sea lettuce, pieces of kelp and of a cylindrical rubbery green alga known as "dead man's fingers."

The students identified the creatures, measured them, and returned the small lobsters to the water. They sorted the rest of the catch to take some of them home for dinner, and others back to the school laboratory to preserve and dissect. They made two trawls that day and by the time they returned to the dock, everyone was happily exhausted.

"This was fabulous," Alice told Bruce as she prepared to leave the vessel. "Unfortunately, I've got to go as soon as we finish docking."

"Can't you stay, at least long enough to have a drink with me? Maybe Dawson would even join us," Bruce replied.

"I'm committed to something this evening, or I just might have accepted your kind invitation to add another couple of hours to this perfectly wonderful day."

The boat bumped gently against the side of the dock, announcing they had landed. The mate was tying off the dock lines. The students began to unload their gear and their catch. Alice turned back to Bruce, "Thank you again, sir. I'll live on the memory of this day for quite a while."

Bruce smiled at her. "Not for too long, I hope, before we see each other again and have another adventure."

She continued the banter as she stepped onto the dock, and turned to wave to Captain Dawson, now supervising the cleanup in progress on deck.

"Don't waste your time. He's already got a girlfriend," Bruce shouted, laughing. Alice smiled and waved at him again. "And I've got you," Bruce thought to himself.

\*\*\*

"How much ambiguity can you handle?" Carrie grilled Alice at their session that same evening.

"Your life is blown apart at the seams and everything is up for grabs. Aren't you the least bit concerned about anything? Do you think it's all going to just serendipitously fall into place?"

Alice laughed at Carrie's earnest expression. "I haven't been waking up in the middle of the night. I've lost my job a couple of times and experienced the possible loss of my child. This is serious, but I have been through worse. My body knows the difference between mortal and venial threats. I'll be concerned when anxiety sets in and the cold sweats begin."

Alice recounted her job search and consideration of other opportunities she might look for if she could not find employment in her chosen field. Reconciling with Ralph would never be the answer to her situation. She made her decision knowing full well the risks she would have to run. She was at ease about that. She would keep right on working the issues and was confident she would be just fine.

The conversation continued with a description of the day of trawling with Bruce and the students. Alice was glowing by the time she finished her story. Carrie decided to probe the relationship. She asked Alice about her feelings for Bruce.

Alice readily admitted to some indecision. On the one hand, he had helped and encouraged her to become a biologist. That experience had a tremendous psychological impact on her—she felt it as if it were a homecoming. She emerged from it as a confident woman at peace with herself. On the other hand, Bruce from time to time showed interest in a far different relationship than Alice was willing to allow. Whenever things heated up between them, a cooling off period usually followed, then the cycle of their friendship would resume.

Carrie reminded her of the "facilitator" hypothesis they discussed earlier, and cautioned, "A facilitator is not necessarily a friend. Facilitators take no prisoners, but they can serve as guides to the next phase." She asked Alice, if Eric were a facilitator for her in the positive sense, helping to ease her transition, how would she characterize Bruce? After a few moments' hesitation, Alice described Bruce as a hazardous friend. She had always felt that about him. If Bruce's behavior toward her ever got out of hand, it could mean real trouble for Alice. He tested her in ways that were simultaneously interesting and annoying. Nevertheless he helped her at very important junctures, both personally and in her professional development. She would always be thankful for that. Alice felt challenged by him, but never overwhelmed. His was such a magnetic personality that she was always very aware of him when they were together. She was always attentive to his moves.

\*\*\*

Much later that same evening, after she finished her own dinner and once again left Ralph's wrapped in plastic on the kitchen counter, Alice went out into the yard with a glass of wine and sat near the water's edge. The moon had risen above a nearly full tide casting a highway of light across the harbor. Ducks floating nearby cackled to each other in soft contented voices. For a while, as the birds murmured in the background, she thought about Brad and how they had made love, whispering and caressing each other. Tears trickled down her cheek. After all this time, his loss still had the power to summon bereavement. Love for him still burned in her heart.

Then she recalled the day when construction of her home was nearing completion and Ralph yelled at her that he couldn't afford to live there. She again felt the sting of that personal rejection. When he refused to acknowledge the beauty of the world surrounding their home, she felt that as a dismissal of the very roots of her existence.

She sat in silence looking out over the rippling surface as the moon continued to ascend, and thought how fast the earth must rotate for the moon's position in the sky to change so rapidly. As it disappeared behind some wispy clouds, it lighted them with a diffuse ivory glow.

Everything that she ever imagined was hers detached and evaporated. Disconnected from all things of material importance on the earth, Alice was pared and honed down to basic essence. Emptied, she sat there. She sighed at the heavens, inhaled deeply, and entered the void as pure spirit. Her soul, naked, unembellished, and altogether unremarkable, passed through the eye of the needle. It lasted only the briefest moment, barely a single beat of the heart. It was empty of light and color. No trumpets flourished or cymbals clashed. There was no sound. It was just a vast nothingness. She was there and then she wasn't. The material world waited the merest instant to reclaim her. She was a creature of the clay and for but a moment her spirit soared forth. The clay awaited her return, and gently welcomed her back. Earthy tentacles reached out for her, attached and drew her in, but did not engulf her in quite the same way as before.

***

When she opened the attic to finally divide the boxes into "his" and "hers", and repack her things into the clothes closets in her bedroom where she could easily reach and organize the stuff to be consigned, like the wedding gifts hardly ever used over the years, Alice first saw that the rifle and boxes of ammunition were missing. It gave her a start.

Ralph concealed his intrusion so well that Alice couldn't tell when he had done it. She wasn't used to him acting with stealth; this revelation that he could, made her uncomfortable. She wondered where the weapon now lay hidden. Was it still in the house? She spent some tense moments imagining where he might have put the rifle, checked in those places and did not find it. She wondered if it were not in the house, where had he taken it?

In other circumstances, she might have believed he placed it somewhere on board the boat. But now that the vessel was under a sale agreement, it was only a matter of time before a marine surveyor hired by the buyer would appear at the boatyard to inspect every inch of the craft from stem to stern. It was not likely he would try to hide the rifle in the boat.

He might have taken it to Penelope's apartment. Alice recalled the arsenal that Pen's husband had collected and displayed in their home. She thought that Pen might be willing to store Ralph's stuff—but what if he was planning to use it? Alice was concerned about why Ralph felt he had to secretly creep into a packed attic space, right to the very back, remove the weapon and ammunition, and then replace things so carefully that she wouldn't notice the disturbance. She decided to tell Phoebe about the absent weapon and ask her opinion.

At first Alice was anxious that Ralph would detect that she had been back into the attic and moved her boxes out. After mulling it over, she decided he probably wouldn't notice, now that the weapon had been removed. He wouldn't have to bother to look in there again. Nothing else urgent to him remained in any of the boxes already packed up—it was all just stuff like mementos of his youth, family photos, and other items of a similar nature.

It continued to nag at her mind that he had done something stealthy and possibly threatening. She hadn't expected it of him. With or without reason, she could come to fear what he might do next. There was so much more about him that she had not expected now beginning to surface. She still couldn't decide whether it was a real threat to her that he had this weapon and she no longer knew where he concealed it.

\*\*\*

A couple of evenings later, with Ralph now away on his fishing expedition, Eric called to ask how she was doing. Alice told him of the missing rifle. They spoke for a while; then Eric's voice became serious. "Alice, you should bring this to your lawyer's attention immediately. You should also tell your daughter, whether or not you truly believe that her father would try to use a weapon to threaten you."

Eric's concern for her, even though it came from the other side of the continent, made Alice feel better. Observing her from the sidelines, he often helped her to put things into perspective. She depended on his insightfulness, and would again follow his advice.

Ralph was away, Eric had called, and Alice felt expansive with the full space of the house available to her without the sound of another person breathing. She luxuriated in that. For once, she could relax in her own home. Alice had begun a job search which now seemed as if it might bear fruit in the not too distant future. She didn't want a job offer coinciding with the divorce settlement. She didn't want to chance anything being re-opened once she and Ralph reached an agreement. It was now an easier task for her to do the paperwork for the coming settlement meeting, believing that her life would be happier and more structured when this was all over.

\*\*\*

It was another perfectly peaceful day. Just as she was leaving for her office, she heard the phone. Rather than let the call go to the voicemail, she picked it up. It was Bruce, calling to tell her about a sad event. Several years earlier, Alice was reunited with a friend from one of her biology classes. Bruce was their professor, and advisor to both women. He believed more than the others in keeping in touch with "his" alumni. A group had met for lunch. Serena placed herself next to Alice. After some time spent chatting, Serena tapped her on the wrist and said, "I want your life."

Alice had recoiled from that. What did she really know about Alice's life? What Serena saw was the surface—the career woman, with family responsibilities seemingly under control. She envied Alice's perceived freedom.

Serena was married to a former Army officer who, she told Alice, tended to be quite authoritarian. She frequently had to make peace between him and their two sons, both "flower children." It seemed the classic example of offspring who chose their identities based on the exact opposite of what a strong parent represented to them.

Tragedy just now struck that family. Serena's younger son was dead of an overdose of drugs. Alice recalled that earlier conversation, remembering her own reaction to it. She was rocked to her very soul by the thought of what she had been through during the trying episodes of Melanie's illness. That had been awful, but she had not lost her daughter, and Alice was grateful beyond words. Bruce was telling her about the funeral, two days away, and a wake being held the next day. The alumni group would all go to show their love and support for Serena. Alice was the last on his list to call, and he was glad he reached her. Would she be able to attend either the wake or funeral? Of course she would do that. She would be at the wake on the following evening and at the funeral mass. This must be a terrible blow to Serena. Alice offered a sad prayer for her.

The next evening, Alice got to the funeral home, saw the mourning family, cried as she held Serena close, and then knelt by the closed casket of a young man too soon departed from life. The many neighbors present, as well as family and friends still continuing to arrive expanded the crowd inside the building. The room was filled to overflowing. The casket lay surrounded by phalanxes of flower arrangements exuding an almost overpowering perfume. Alice felt the atmosphere turning uncomfortably warm. The crowd of jostling bodies made it hard to move or to breathe. Bruce appeared at her elbow and asked if she could stop for a drink with him afterward. She barely had time to accept his invitation before he again disappeared into the crowd.

As soon as the priest finished his brief service people began to leave by two's and three's. The fresh air outside the building served to revive Alice. Bruce was standing nearby waiting for her to appear. They decided on a meeting place and left the funeral home.

"I can't believe this has happened," Bruce began as they sipped their drinks. "He was a bright, promising young man. Serena wanted me to mentor him, and I thought I'd have another success story on my hands. Sure didn't expect this."

Alice was quiet. What was there to say? She had been so fortunate with the way Melanie had turned her illness around. Her mind wandered for a few moments on that theme. Bruce continued to talk, and Alice finally tuned back in to hear him ask if she would ever change her mind about him as a lover?

Alice was no longer the young woman she had been when Bruce first asked her this question. Then, the answer to such invitations had always been an immediate and unequivocal "No." In midlife such things are no longer automatically categorized as "yes" or "no" propositions. The experience of battling her way through various crises left Alice respecting her own vulnerabilities as well as those of others. Bruce had witnessed her change. That drew him closer to her now than he had ever felt himself to be when both of them were younger. As the older, more mature man he had become, he treated that knowledge with deference. Over the years since she first met him, she learned that he had an eye for women, and that mostly he respected the ones he couldn't seduce, however hard he tried. He and Alice were still so connected in their on again/off again friendship that they had preserved their role of confidants to each other. Bruce never abused her trust, nor she his. That's how things remained as the years passed. This time Alice didn't respond to him as she always had. He noted her hesitation and let her take her time to answer him.

Maybe she was more upset by the missing weapon than she thought. Maybe it was the effect of the alcohol on her, or a combination of that and everything else that she had endured in the previous months. The proximity of Bruce's primal male presence radiated as if to envelop her in a cocoon of safety, and she began to feel lightheaded. She had lived for years without the contentment that she had once known from being cherished by a man. What was happening to her now? The intimacy of their conversation, his arm casually lying along the back of her chair, the warm fragrance that emanated from his skin shrouded her in a kind of magical aura. In another time or place, Alice might have chided him for trying to take advantage of her and make him back off. But the need that she had denied so often now prevented her from doing that. Quite simply, Alice wanted to be held and Bruce was perfectly willing to oblige her.

"Alice," Bruce spoke softly into her ear, "I know I can make you feel the way a woman deserves to feel when she's with a man. Won't you let me do that for you? We've been friends for a long time. I care very much about you and I only want what's best for you."

Alice's mind was racing. "Why not? What else could happen, after all? What if my life were over tomorrow, would I regret that I didn't take this opportunity to be loved just once more?" Bruce's attentions were a part of the life she once had. That was a whole separate existence outside her marriage. On the days she traveled to the college and was on her own, she felt as carefree as she had been before she met Ralph. She was free for those hours and days, thoroughly enjoying her independence. In spite of the hard work required to earn a degree, it had felt to her like guilty pleasure. Those were possibly the most carefree moments of her life, and all that time she had remained true to Ralph. She was still married, but that was about to end. There was no longer any point to considering a show of faithfulness, was there? If she did sleep with Bruce now, it would be something that was a long time coming. How would she feel about herself afterward if she did give in to how willing and desirous her body now felt? He was kissing her ear, breathing softly into it. She felt her blood race. They left the bar together, his arm around her waist. "You won't regret it," he whispered to her. "I love you."

They drove to Bruce's small house. He bought it soon after his own divorce some years earlier. His wife caught him with another woman; he was unable to convince her that it wasn't serious, and she divorced him. Perhaps Bruce told her the same story too many times for it to still sound credible. Alice knew that much about his history, but somehow it didn't matter now. Her own divorce loomed large. Her pain because of Ralph's treatment of her still throbbed like an open wound. Bruce's tenderness in loving her throughout that night brought her the balm she needed to salve her injuries. He was a practiced lover, and did have a genuine liking, even to the point of love, for Alice. As the tenderness flowed from him, she relaxed into his arms.

They sat together at the funeral on the next morning. Bruce was very solicitous of her. Alice wore the same clothes she had on the evening before, but all attention was on the service, the casket, and Serena, who threatened to dissolve into tears at the least provocation. It was moving and sad. When it was all over, they left together. Then Alice went home.

As wonderful as the night with Bruce had been, Alice felt that something had been lost. Driving home, she recalled Ros's experience. She now understood how powerful a draw the intimate attentions of a man could be in a situation like divorce where a woman was so emotionally exposed. Alice acknowledged that she was no exception to that rule. Bruce had seen her helplessness and expertly maneuvered around her defenses. Alice was shaken by the thought that after the love she shared with Brad, she could ever again be captivated by any man's charm. But there it was. She was disarmed by her own human weakness. She hadn't set out to have an affair with Bruce, or even to have this one night stand. Strangely for her, she did not feel any regrets that she gave in to Bruce's advances. She thought it would have been a far more terrible thing if she had altogether lost the ability to do so.

*\*\**

Ralph returned too soon for Alice's comfort. She lamented that the breathing space, such as it had been, was now ended. She had become accustomed to having the house to herself, not worrying about when he might come through the door. Seeing him again reminded her of how important it would be to reach a settlement agreement as quickly as possible. In the aftermath of her night with Bruce, it also reminded her of all that Ralph had withheld from her throughout their marriage. That made her angry and gave her a new source of energy to push ahead. She was to call Phoebe upon Ralph's return so the lawyers could set a date and time for a discussion. However brief, she was grateful to have had the respite.

*\*\**

Alice received her copy of the first letter from Hubert to Phoebe. Finally, here was a sign of something, somewhere being put into motion. The letter led to a first meeting between the divorcing parties and their lawyers. It was held in the County Court House, and lasted an entire day.

Alice was the first to arrive. She sat on a bench in the reception area awaiting Phoebe's appearance. Hubert made a swaggering entrance. He shook hands and exchanged pleasantries with the security guard, a young man who was posted at the scanner in the building's entryway. Alice wondered if the

attorney knew who she was. Phoebe briskly entered the vestibule a few minutes later. Ralph soon followed. They found a
table with four chairs in one of the corridors, and claimed them
for the day. They seated themselves. The attorneys positioned
their briefcases on the table, snapping the lids open into their
opponent's face, and then got to work.

# Ralph

As the lawyers organized their papers, Alice and I stared at each other across the battlefield. The accommodations were smaller than the average kitchen table and chairs; the hallway was so narrow we were all but wedged in together. "Combat at close quarters," I thought.

Hubert cleared his throat and asked Phoebe if the list of household items was still the same, and if there was agreement as to their disposal. Glancing at Alice and seeing her slight nod, Phoebe responded, "Still the same with us."

I should have expected that a meeting like this wasn't going to be especially friendly. But Phoebe came out of the box like a pit bull and caught me and Hubert completely by surprise.

It started off pleasantly enough—"I understand we have an agreement about the division of household goods. That's great. I'd like to go over it to be sure that we are all in accord before we take up the difficult items. But first, I have a question for Ralph."

Hubert was puzzled. "Is it about something on the list?"

"It wasn't on the list. It's a weapon."

Hubert was startled. "Are you implying something about my client?"

"I'm asking where the rifle and ammunition that were stored

130

in the attic went. And now that you mention it, I would like to hear from your client what he intends to do with them." Phoebe clearly enunciated each word.

Hubert admitted that I had never told him about any such thing, and that he and I needed to talk before either of us answered her questions. He gave me a nod and asked Phoebe to excuse us for a few minutes. We walked together down the narrow hallway, Hubert slightly behind me as if positioning his bulk to absorb any words that might pass between us as we went. We found an empty corner and used it as a place to huddle.

"Now tell me what this is all about."

"I have a rifle." I proceeded to explain to him about belonging to a rod and gun club since I had been in high school. I still kept a rifle because I enjoyed shooting targets once in a while, but I hadn't used it in a long time.

"If you weren't using it, then what's so special about this rifle that you kept it in your house all these years?"

"It's an M-1, from when I was in the service. Like a lot of other guys, I bought it after I came off active duty and went into the National Guard. It's been in the attic all along. Alice knew about it. In fact, when she packed up the stuff we had stored there and put everything in boxes, she moved the rifle and the ammo to the back corner."

"So Alice knew you had them, and she knew where they were?"

"Yes, I guess that's right. One day I went looking for them. When I finally found them in back of all the boxes she had piled in there, I took them out of the attic. Then I replaced all the stuff she had stored in front of them. Of course I took them out. I wasn't going to leave them there. They are mine, after all. They're nothing she would ever want."

"Whether or not she would ever want them is not the issue. The issue is whether or not you would ever try to use them on her. So now I have to ask you a question, and you have to be honest about answering. I signed on to represent you for a divorce, nothing else. There will be nothing else, is that right?"

Hubert was adamant. "Do you still have them? Are they still somewhere in the house? If you argue about this, it'll look like you want to be able to use them to threaten Alice. I don't want to have to defend you for that. Let's not complicate the issue. The divorce is enough."

I was amazed by all of this. What was the big deal? Of course I would never even think about hurting Alice. She's the mother of my kid, for Heaven's sake. I thought Hubert was being a whole lot over-dramatic about the rifle. But I thought that now I had to assure him that I had taken the stuff out of the house, so I said it was somewhere in my sister's house, probably in her storage closet.

Hubert wanted a note from Pen verifying what I just said. I agreed to ask but was doubtful Pen would go along with that. I asked Hubert, "What turned this into front page news? It doesn't amount to a hill of beans." Hubert insisted it was important because Alice was obviously concerned enough to mention it to Phoebe. Therefore she was obliged to bring it up at our meeting. "The point is," Hubert explained, "now we all know that you have possession of a weapon and ammunition. No one has yet suggested that you might use it, just that you have it somewhere. Wherever it is, Alice feels it's a threat to her."

What a stupid mess. Alice was nervous because she knew I had the rifle and she didn't know where it was. All the years I had guns in the house I don't remember her ever taking a census. It's not like I did anything wrong or illegal. Hubert gave me the Dutch uncle treatment. If anything happened to Alice, it would be curtains for me. The lawyers would have to go to the police and tell them about this. The police wouldn't bother to look any further for a guilty party. I hadn't thought about that angle.

"Look, I can't be your lawyer if you don't come clean with me about stuff like this. You didn't tell me you had a weapon in the house where you are still living with your wife who's divorcing you. The problem is," he carefully articulated each word, "angry spouses have been known to use weapons in very emotional situations. This would look terrible for you if Phoebe ever decided to bring it up before the judge. It doesn't matter if Alice knows you have it. What does matter right now is that you can go back in there and prove to Phoebe that it is not in your immediate possession and does not represent a threat to her client."

Hubert was pretty persuasive on that count, so we went back to the table. I said that the rifle and ammunition were in the possession of my sister, and I had no idea what she had done with them. I apologized to Alice for not telling her that I had removed them. She told me how startled she had been to find the stuff gone, and that bothered her enough to tell Phoebe. She thought about telling Melanie, but decided not to alarm her if there was no reason to. Hubert added that I offered to ask Pen for a note that she agreed to store the rifle and ammo for me until I knew for sure where I was going to be living. I caught Alice's smirk.

Then I thought it would be interesting to mention that Alice had also once handled firearms. Maybe I thought that would make me feel better, but it didn't. Both lawyers immediately turned to her and asked for an explanation. She said her experience was confined to target shooting with a 22-calibre rifle. That was a very long time ago. She did not own a weapon, and never had. Then she laughed and said, "Nice try for a diversion, Ralph."

I finally realized I needed to get them off that subject, so I mentioned there was something else I wanted to make sure was out in the open. "While we're still in the confessional, telling each other about things, I thought I'd best bring up the purchase and sales agreement for the boat." I apologized for not telling Alice when it needed to be signed and just made a clean breast of that whole thing. At least Hubert already knew that story so he didn't have to drag me outside for another trip to the woodshed. I finally finished making all my confessions. This had used up the entire morning. It was just about time for lunch. We left our stuff on the table and took a break. As we got up to leave, Hubert asked Phoebe whether she had any more surprises for him. "I hope not," she said. She was smooth.

***

As we ate our sandwiches, Hubert checked in with his office to see if there were any messages. Except for having to return a couple of quick calls, he was pretty quiet. Maybe I was his only big deal for the moment. Good for me. This gave me a little time to think about the rifle. Actually, it was still inside the house, in the attic above the master—now Alice's—bedroom. I did not expect Alice knew that. I never thought about it as being a threat to her, but now after all that discussion, I could understand where they were coming from. I wasn't able to bring myself to admit to Hubert the thing was still in the house, so I'd have to sneak back in, retrieve it, bring it to Pen's and hope she'd actually be willing to cooperate with me. That was going to cost me—the question was, how much? Would Pen write a note for me? If not, maybe I could at least get her to call Hubert and reassure him. No one could force her to put anything on paper, and I doubted that she would be willing to do it.

Hubert and I spent some time reviewing the finances and talking about things like health insurance, pensions, savings and checking accounts. I thought it was important to go through who paid for what—since, over the course of my marriage, I paid for nearly everything when it came to the house, supporting the family and all that. Compared to what I contributed, Alice didn't provide squat. After I had let off some steam about it, Hubert told me to leave it alone.

"Don't waste your time. This is a joint property state. The judge will be looking for a 50/50 settlement. Anything too far off the mark guarantees he'll start to ask questions. He won't especially care to hear what you just said to me." I felt deflated.

Before we went back to the table in the hallway, Hubert indulged in a little gallows humor. "Remember the conversation we had about that cemetery plot?" When he saw me nod, he said, "Don't mention it." He was right. I could just see it. First I have a weapon that threatens her, then I have a brand new family burial plot I just bought, and I offer her the chance to sign the papers so she can be buried there. How idiotic would that be? Even I knew better than to touch that third rail.

\*\*\*

When we got back to the table, Alice and Phoebe were laughing at something. I took that to mean the atmosphere had lightened up a bit. I hoped it was a good sign for the afternoon's discussion.

Hubert began on the aggressive side. Now that the morning was out of the way, he figured he could start out fresh. He shot himself in the foot when he said something to Phoebe about conceding to her with the promise we made about the weapon, and now we were looking for something in return.

She shot right back at him and it wasn't pretty. She asked if he thought it was a concession for him to promise his client would not attempt to threaten or commit violence to her client. She raised her voice, "He is still living in the same house with her, Hubert. Don't you think that's just a little bit intimidating to her without some weapon being brandished about? I can ask the judge to get him out of there. I don't need your help to do that."

Hubert cleared his throat and nervously restated, "I'm only trying to say—however clumsily, I do admit—that we want to achieve an amicable result here this afternoon."

"Fine," Phoebe snapped. "Let's try to do that."

It sounded like some kind of soap opera. It was very theatrical. But it was dead serious, for me at least.

# Alice

Her head was pounding by four o'clock. Not much progress had been made. The judge sent a clerk to ask if they were nearly ready to go to the courtroom.

Phoebe said tersely, "We're still trying to reach agreement."

"The judge says he'll wait another half-hour if that will help," the clerk replied.

"It doesn't look like we'll make it today. Tell the judge we thank him for his patience, but we don't want to keep him waiting. We're too far away from a settlement."

Alice was depressed by all of the bickering. She listened to Ralph yell about not touching his retirement savings; about how much Alice had in hers; about her nerve in asking for the house; about how Alice spent all his money; about how she wrote checks out of his checking account, and now he was overdrawn. Hubert then demanded that since Alice's name was on the checks, she pay half Ralph's debt. Alice had reacted, of course. Phoebe told Hubert they'd discuss the matter. Hubert then remarked that Ralph was covered under Alice's health insurance plan, and demanded that he be continued. Ralph looked pleased when he heard Hubert say that.

"Ralph has only to call his company's Human Resources

office and ask to be put on their health plan. That's all it would take for him to have his own insurance. He doesn't need to be on mine," Alice demanded angrily. "Besides, my job is temporary and I am now searching for a new one. I can't provide health insurance for him. I don't know where I'll be or whether I'll have any kind of health benefits at all. He's the one with the steady employment and can easily provide his own coverage."

Phoebe backed her up. "Don't be ridiculous, Hubert. Ralph can take care of that for himself."

\*\*\*

The courthouse was closing at five, so Phoebe offered to adjourn their meeting to her office across the street. They gathered up their things and walked out of the building, each pair in earnest conversation. The lawyers had their copies of Alice's and Ralph's financial statements to review. Settling into separate meeting rooms in Phoebe's office, each duo could talk privately about what they were willing to offer and what they wanted to withhold.

Alice sat staring at her and Ralph's financial statements lying side by side on the table in front of her. Something was not quite right. How could she appear to have so great a proportion of their joint wealth? All at once, the answer caught her eye. Ralph had not reported his retirement investments. Once included, that adjusted the picture to one that made sense, based on their individual earnings and savings. She called Phoebe's attention to that.

Phoebe grabbed the statement and burst into the office being used by Hubert and Ralph. "Look here," she demanded. "Your client has not even reported all his financial assets." Ralph blanched at the tirade. Hubert held his breath. Disregarding his expression, Phoebe continued, "I want to see a most recent, up-to-date statement as to what the number is that belongs in this line—deferred savings for retirement. Right now it's empty. That is not a complete report of your client's assets."

The color returned to Ralph's face. Hubert exhaled heavily, angered by the intrusion. "We'll get the statement for you," he agreed. "But I have a question for you as well. Where's your client's retirement account from her present job?"

"I'll get that for you," Phoebe retorted. "She's only worked there for about a year. We're not talking about anything in the same league as Ralph's omission. But you're right."

Alice was surprised when Phoebe pointed out her similar oversight. Quickly she scanned her statement and found that missing. "I'll send it you tomorrow," she agreed.

"Don't feel you have to rush. Ralph won't get his statement to me for at least another week. Then we can talk again. You'll be okay. Don't be too concerned about all this. We'll have to try for another court date, but the judge won't consider it until we have an agreement. We'll have to have another sit-down with them," she nodded toward the room where Hubert and Ralph were meeting.

"Is there anything else we need to do this evening?"

"Doesn't make sense to try with the data we now know is missing from the financial statements. It just occurred to me— what about that checking account? Are you willing to take half that debt?"

Alice replied, "I don't ever recall signing a signature card for that account. If I didn't, then I am not a co-owner of it or of the debt. Tomorrow I'll go to the bank and get the answer to that question."

"Call me when you find out. Meanwhile, I'll tell them we're ready to adjourn until we can all find a day and time to sit and discuss the issues some more. I'll set that up with Hubert and let you know." Phoebe smiled at her. "Don't worry, Alice. We'll get there. Maybe it'll be sooner than you think."

\*\*\*

Wearily, Alice entered the dark house. The red light that indicated a message from an earlier call glowed in the interior dimness. Turning on the desk light, she picked up the phone, retrieved the message and listened to Bruce's recorded voice inviting her to attend the fish auction with some students and faculty. Alice had always wanted to go, but wasn't able to while she had been a student. After the night she and Bruce made love, she knew that as much as she wanted an opportunity to repeat that experience with him, she couldn't go through with it. What if he saw her acceptance of this invitation as the signal that she would be compliant?

Recalling that night, she was surprised at how gentle he had been with her, and how lovingly he held her afterward, the pleasant warmth of his body and the smell of his skin enveloping her as he whispered affectionately into her ear. Each time she thought about it, she felt the power of the experience, and once more grasped how empty and arid the long years of her life with Ralph had been. She had missed this kind of attentive loving, and now wanted more of it, just as anyone who had been rescued from starvation couldn't get their fill of food. It felt like there could never be enough love to make up for what Ralph had withheld from her over the years. But, like the remedy for hunger, receiving a sudden bounty of what had been missing was not the best road to recovery. She was still surprised at herself for what she had done. Realizing how much was at stake, Alice knew she must end this affair now before it became destructive to what she needed to achieve for her future by divorcing Ralph.

Alice saw Bruce's invitation as a double-edged sword. She was enticed to return to a time and place where she was free of care in an environment where she felt grounded. It was a powerful draw. Bruce knew very well what he was doing. So far as seeing the fish auction, she decided that would now be her chance to talk with him and end this affair before it became any more rooted in her life. She was so needy and had so easily succumbed to Bruce that she worried she might never be able to free herself if this went on any longer. She returned his call, leaving him a voice message that accepted and thanked him for his serendipitous invitation.

\*\*\*

Alice knew all about the auction by reputation, but this was her chance to finally experience it for herself. The fishermen were supposed to be very rough on women who tried to intrude on this important daily morning ritual. The only female allowed in the auction hall was a reporter for the local newspaper. The men liked her style. Bruce had a strategy for attending with Alice. The faculty and students were all men. Alice would always be surrounded by them. Their protective behavior would signal that her presence was to be tolerated.

They drove to the fish pier early that morning. It was a slightly overcast day. The long low metal building that housed the auction hall stood on a short pier near the dirt parking lot. Boats newly arrived from the fishing grounds sat at nearby moorings waiting for instructions to unload. Oily water lapped at the wharf pilings as the tide rose inside the harbor. The water exhaled a fishy odor and the air itself seemed torpid with the burden of it.

In an earlier era, the vast surrounding area might have been covered with fish flakes, wooden racks set out to hold cut pieces of salted fish while they dried in the sun. Now it was covered by structures that housed processing plants. Docks extended from the buildings out into the harbor to receive any vessel whose catch was destined for their cutting rooms.

Inside the auction hall, Alice saw a lot of men in dark work clothes milling about. They seemed to be the captains and mates of the fishing boats. Although a soft murmuring sound was audible in the room, no one seemed to be speaking directly to anyone else. From time to time the men glanced at the blackboard behind the auctioneer where the catches and prices were being recorded. Each entry was followed by a muttered exchange between what must have been the captain and mate of the vessel whose catch was then being bid. No one else seemed to react to the prices. There was only brief acknowledgement when a boatload had been spoken for. Once or twice, Alice overheard terse instructions being given about which dock to bring a certain vessel to for unloading. The auctioneer stood at a podium, looking up from his clipboard, sometimes giving a slight nod, and then making some notes. A couple of men in business suits entered discretely, stood at the back and made slight gestures before leaving separately. The reporter walked about in the room, unremarked, writing into her notebook.

After about fifteen minutes, everyone began to file out of the building. It was over. Alice wondered what had happened. How had all this business been transacted with barely a nod, only a slight indication—movements that must have been detectable to the auctioneer, in spite of the confusion of bodies inside that smoke-filled hall? She looked forward to an explanation once they made their exit.

Approaching the door, her vigilant escorts steered her away from a small group of men deep in some kind of argumentative post mortem, their voices raised, their gestures quick and choppy. As Alice turned in the other direction, she caught sight of a woman who wore a round, black, flat-brimmed hat—like a gaucho hat. From beneath it, long strands of black curly hair descended over a foul weather jacket. She held a cigarillo between her tapered fingers. Observing her closely, Alice saw that the woman had suffered, but her bearing spoke of someone who had overcome great obstacles. The deep strength and authenticity that radiated from her held Alice spellbound. Sensing she was being scrutinized, the woman turned her rumpled face and looked directly at Alice, who couldn't help staring at her. Her face looked as if she had either been in one or more fistfights, or experienced abuse. Whatever it was, it had been so long ago that what must have been the sharper planes of broken bones and bruises had softened into the present landscape of her face. Beneath her jacket, the woman wore dark pants tucked into waterproof work boots. The handle of a long filleting knife protruded from the top of her right boot.

Alice was seized by the thoughts that now flooded her consciousness. In contrast to this woman, whose presence fit in here, Alice felt she was attempting to retreat to things she had now left behind, but that had once provided her with a meaningful context. Her "returns to her roots," as Bruce phrased it, were welcoming and happy. But the places that she journeyed to in the intervening years—where she became a woman who could courageously file for a mid-life divorce—demanded purpose and strength. Alice now recognized she had come closer than she realized to forsaking all that she had labored to achieve. And for what? Simply to have an affair with Bruce? She didn't try to delude herself that it would ever add up to anything more than that. How would it all end? She thought again of her friend Ros, who was so defenseless, and yet summoned the strength to overcome rejection. At the time she heard Ros's story, Alice never imagined herself as being someone who could fall for such a man. But here she was, doing the very same thing. The fact that it was Bruce, whom she knew so well, made it even less comprehensible to her. If Alice had realized she must act, and found the courage to follow through, why would she now squander everything by embarking on an affair with him? It was enough that she had memories of a time when her life had felt fulfilled and been much happier. This was not the time to indulge in reliving the past, or for trying to reinvent it to define her future, but for facing what she knew was to come. After all, she was responsible for setting it all into motion. She now fully recognized the futility of continuing to retreat to a portion of her life from which she had long ago departed.

Gratitude now spread across Alice's features as her eyes once again sought the mysterious woman's face. Her very presence seemed both a blessing and an absolution. She stood, watching the changing expressions that flickered across Alice's face, as if aware of her deepest thoughts. As Alice's eyes refocused on the woman, she gave a quick nod and then turned away and disappeared into the crowd.

None of the men paid any particular attention to the woman, although their body language spoke to their awareness of her presence. If no one so much as ventured a look in her direction, that meant they knew who she was, and that she was someone they did not customarily approach or address without good reason. The men were very curious about Alice, and made that obvious with their turned heads, prolonged stares and terse comments. That mysterious woman obviously belonged there.

Alice couldn't begin to imagine who she could be. Her clothing suggested she might do physical work, but her demeanor was that of someone who was accustomed to being in charge. With such an authoritative stance, was she captain of a vessel? Did she own one of the fish processing plants? Maybe she was a union leader. Alice could not tell what she was doing there, but it excited her to so unexpectedly see this woman, so confident and self-possessed, in the middle of what Alice understood to be a completely male-dominated kingdom. Alice asked Bruce who the woman was, but he appeared not to have seen her. He looked slowly and deliberately around the now-dispersing crowd, but she had gone. Bruce asked the others if they had seen her, but no one else had. Was she a figment of Alice's imagination? She hoped not. It was suddenly important to her that this enigmatic figure was real. Alice could leave her the mystery of her identity.

She clearly recognized that opportunities to be with Bruce were primarily chances to escape from the grim process of her divorce. His attention made her feel desirable and womanly. She did accept Bruce as a lover for that one beautiful night, and she would treasure that as his unique gift to her, but these interludes with him must now come to an end.

When Alice and Bruce left the fish auction, they decided to stop for coffee. They talked about Alice's divorce, Bruce's plans for the remainder of the academic year, how Serena was holding up after the loss of her son, anything other than their night together. It seemed they both wanted to avoid that topic. Their conversation began to wind down as they left the coffee shop. Bruce drove Alice back to her car. As they were saying goodbye, Bruce's handsome face assumed a troubled look. "Alice, are you all right? Let's go off into the dunes for the rest of the afternoon and just make love. Our night together was so magnificent."

Alice laughed. "I wanted to talk to you about that, but I

hardly knew where to begin. You were wonderful and taught me what having you as a lover could mean to me. But I can't have an affair with you. I have too much at stake with my divorce. You've been through it too, so you have to understand why I'm saying this to you now. I don't want things to end badly between us. We've been too good as friends for too many years."

He smiled at her. "I have to agree with you, but I don't want to. Alice, what we did was right. You were down and you needed to know for a fact that you're one of the sexiest women I ever met in my life, no matter how Ralph has treated you. He's a moron. He threw you away. Could you blame me for trying to catch you? I mean, come on, Alice. There you are, all L.L. Bean on the outside, and inside, a true Victoria's Secret girl. How am I supposed to resist that?"

His resounding laugh and close hug made her chuckle. He understood. She knew that would be the case. He had done his best to argue her out of her decision, at least for this round, and she knew he was anything but a quitter. "Call me when you're ready," were his parting words to her.

If she had gone off with a lover into the dunes, it would not have given her such deliverance as she experienced at the sight of that mysterious woman who stood before her as a genuine survivor. For a moment, Alice read that same recognition on her face and saw it in her gestures. That told Alice she too had achieved an authenticity of her own, as well as the recognition that her life was no longer an appendage of Ralph's.

# Ralph

I had to get that rifle and those two boxes of ammo out of the house, but how was I going to manage it? Alice works so close by she can come home for lunch. That meant I either had to come back to the house in the morning after she left, or show up after she returned to the office for the afternoon. Since nobody else knew the rifle was there, I could choose a time when I could be sure she wouldn't be around—or so I thought. It sounded easier than it turned out to be. A couple of days after our lengthy spell in the hallway at the courthouse, I thought I saw my chance. Bruce invited her to go to the fish auction and that meant she'd leave early in the morning and be gone most of the day.

At the last minute, I had to go to the office for an early morning staff meeting, so I left the house soon after Alice did. I thought I had most of the day to accomplish my mission, so I wasn't especially bothered by that. I didn't plan to spend more than a couple of minutes in the attic. In fact, I could reach the rifle and the ammunition boxes right from the opening, so it would be a quick and easy job. Once I had everything, I planned to take it to Pen's place and ask her to store it for me. Then the facts would match what I had told Hubert.

At the office I had to spend some time on the phone with

clients, and then I had to answer a couple of unexpected calls about other business, so it was late morning before I finally got back to the house. I went into Alice's bedroom, opened the closet door and shoved the hatch to the attic aside. I lifted myself up so my head and shoulders were inside the attic space and felt around where I had put the rifle and ammo boxes. I couldn't feel anything there. Were the rifle and ammo gone? I turned on the attic light and went all the way up. I looked around, feeling beneath the insulation in case the stuff had shifted. I was not mistaken—there was nothing there. I was shocked. I was sure I put them there. Maybe I only thought I had. I was sure no one could have taken them. No one else knew they were there.

I went down again through the opening, through the closet and into the hallway. I decided that I'd check the other storage space, the one Alice was using. I opened that up, pulled out the boxes in the front and crawled into it, moving cartons aside and shoving them behind me toward the opening. I went all the way back to the corner where the rifle and ammo had been before I took them out. There was nothing there either. I thought I heard the front door open and close. By then I was nearly in a panic so I started to make my way out, shoving boxes around. I heard the door again. As I pulled myself out of the attic space and into the hallway, I could hear someone downstairs. "Who's there?" I called.

"Who's asking?" was the response. Alice stood at the foot of the stairs in front of the open front door. I was shaking—with relief that it was her and with embarrassment at being caught.

"What the hell is going on here?"

"I guess I owe you an explanation."

"I'd say you do."

Under the circumstances, I couldn't lie to her. So I asked her to sit down with me in the living room and I would explain the situation. "I can't blame you if you don't trust me," I began. "After the discussion I had with Hubert at the courthouse the other day, I knew I had to make things right, that is, to make them the way I said they were. I never intended to threaten you or frighten you about the rifle. I want you to know that. For God's sake, how could I? Did you really imagine I would?"

"Ralph, I spent every weekend going through the stuff in that attic, separating your things from mine, and packing them away in boxes. All that time you were out having fun with your friends. That rifle and those boxes of ammunition were there all summer long."

"What can I say? I know you were working hard to organize that stuff. I should have helped, but I didn't."

"I put the rifle in the back, along with the ammunition boxes, and packed your things on one side and mine on the other as I worked my way back to the opening. Then I knew that stuff was out of the way. I expected it would still be there when we finally unpacked that space and you took out all your things. Imagine how I felt on the day I opened that attic, saw everything had been moved around and then discovered the rifle and ammunition were gone. That made me sick to my stomach."

"Alice, I'm sorry. I should have told you that I was taking it out of the house. And that's what I should have done—take it all the way out of the house right then. When I saw the attic all packed full and no sign of my rifle, I had to go looking to see if it was still there. Once I found it, I just went ahead, took it out, and replaced the boxes just as I'd found them."

"Where did you put the rifle?"

"I had planned to ask Pen to keep it for me until the divorce was all over. I needed a place to keep it until I had the chance to talk to her, so I put it into the attic above the master bedroom. I figured that was such a tough place for you to get up into that you would never try to store anything there. I thought it was a good hiding place."

"You were right. I never would have thought about it. So where is the rifle now?"

"I honestly don't know. It's not where I put it in the attic, and it isn't in the place you were using. It's gone. I don't understand how. We're the only ones in this house, aren't we?"

"Melanie has a key, but she's hardly ever here anymore, and she's just left for school in Pennsylvania."

"The house hasn't been burglarized. So where is the rifle?"

"Ralph, that's a question for you to answer. How should I know? You just told me you took it out of a hiding place that I knew about and put it somewhere that I would never have looked for it, so I'm a little concerned here about how truthful you're being with me. We'll have to tell the lawyers what you have just told me. I'm very nervous about that weapon being hidden somewhere in my house. I want it out of here and you with it. Enough is enough. Do I have to get a court order before I can feel safe in my own home?"

"I wish you wouldn't overreact to this."

"This is hardly overreacting. What would you do if you were in my shoes?"

"I don't know, Alice. I'm stymied. I really don't have the rifle. How could it just disappear?"

"You'd best put on your thinking cap, Ralph. I have to go back to the office for a couple of hours. When I come home, I hope you'll have found it. I want to see that thing leave my house with my own eyes. I'm going to let Phoebe know what's happened."

If she told me she was going to call Phoebe, it was a warning for me to call Hubert. What one of them knows, the other soon finds out—especially if it's something that looks like big trouble for me. I know how much Hubert hates being jumped by Phoebe when he's not prepared for it. Later, Hubert told me that Phoebe wanted to call the police but had no grounds to tell them that I had done anything illegal. He said both women felt threatened by the so-called "menace of the missing weapon." He said those were Phoebe's exact words. Where and when, and under what circumstances, would it ever show up again? I wanted to know the answer, maybe even more than anyone else. It goes without saying that I was pretty rattled by this. How could that stuff be gone? I had it all in my hands not that long ago. Was Alice trying to play a head game with me? She seemed pretty upset, but maybe she's better at acting than I ever gave her credit for. If that was the case, why would she be getting Phoebe involved like this?

I was supposed to meet Bunny for a drink. Now I thought I might get there a little earlier, before she arrived at the bar.

\*\*\*

"Ralph, I have never heard anything like this in my whole life," Bunny responded when I told her about the missing rifle. "It can't have happened by magic. What if Alice has it? Would she try to use it on you?"

"You think Alice would try to shoot me?"

"Stranger things have happened. What if she shot you dead and then told the cops she thought you were an intruder? Ever think of that angle?"

"Alice doesn't have the rifle. She couldn't have known where it was. Even if she did, there was no way that she could get at it without a lot of trouble. Besides, she had her chance when she was packing those boxes and the rifle would have been handy for her, compared to where I had just put it. Then, she called her lawyer to tell her about it being gone. To just out-and-out accuse Alice of taking it—and taking it because she was planning to shoot me with it—wouldn't add up."

"Well then, if you really think it wasn't her, who else has a key to your house?"

"Melanie is the only other person, but she just left for college in Pennsylvania. After all she's been through just the sight of the rifle would be enough to freak her out. Besides, there's no reason for her to go poking around in the attic."

We sat there sipping our drinks, hoping for a sudden resolution to the questions of who, what and why.

"Ralph, you're a nervous wreck. What if they call the police? You'd better be sure Hubert's covered if they do that."

I knew she was right. I said I'd call Hubert again first thing in the morning. I didn't look forward to that at all.

# Melanie

It was a pleasant day, and Melanie had just finished packing up to leave the apartment she shared with a friend, and go off to school in Pennsylvania. She was looking forward to making another beginning. This time she'd concentrate on barn management, which would be a combination of riding classes and general business skills. Alice encouraged her, saying that whatever it took for her to get an academic degree was just fine.

Melanie was ready to leave, except that at the last minute she decided she wanted to take her Teddy bear collection with her. She kept them close by during her illness. They were her bulwark against pain. Some time after Stan moved her back to her parents' house, she was finally able to store them in the attic. Up above her bedroom, they were still close by. She thought of it as a little Heaven, full of her own special benevolent saints, kindly offering protection. Maybe she wanted them for the comfort they gave her from the time she was a little girl. Maybe she didn't want to leave this fragile piece of her life behind in her parents' embattled home.

She drove to their house and let herself in the door. Once again she checked her room for anything else she might have forgotten. Finally she decided to go up into the attic above what was now her mother's bedroom and retrieve the Teddy bears. They were still sitting up there in bags, where she had put them some months earlier. Now they would once again be free to see the light of day.

She removed the items in the closet, made sure the bottom and top shelves were placed so she could stand on them to remove the hatch and then push herself through. When she had done that, she saw that her bags were far enough from the opening that she would have to climb all the way up into the attic to retrieve them.

Melanie pulled herself up, stood and reached for the bags. Looking down, she was horrified to see her father's rifle and two boxes of ammunition directly at her feet. The rifle seemed to be pointed toward the ceiling right above where her mother's bed was located in the room below.

She grabbed the bags, threw them down through the opening and then followed as quickly as if she were a toboggan going down a run. She had hurt herself years ago. Now that whole emotional context returned with a flood of nausea. She rushed into the bathroom and threw up what felt like the entire contents of her body. Flushing the toilet, she cried. She was horrified by the thought that her father might be planning to use the rifle to hurt her mother. Melanie felt confronted by something completely unimaginable. Mechanically, she seized her bags of Teddy bears, ran down the stairs and out the front door. Then she jammed them into her car.

She gulped in the fresh air, trying to clear her head. Her father had never acted as if he might harbor violent feelings toward her mother, but how well did she really know either of them since the divorce began? She wasn't sure. She pulled out first one cigarette, then a second as she tried to compose herself, and decide what to do next. What if she just put everything back and pretended she had never been there? She was planning to leave for school the next morning. If the rifle did represent a threat to her mother, she wouldn't be there to see it materialize.

No, she decided, that was not what she had to do. She went

back inside the house and dialed Angela's number. Luckily, she was in her office. Melanie was relieved to not encounter either the voicemail or the answering service. "I know we've said good-bye already, but something has just happened that I need to talk to you about." She told Angela about the rifle and ammunition.

"That worries me. I know you're planning to leave soon for school, but if you want to come and see me later this afternoon, I've got a cancellation."

"You've been a great help just to talk to. It was hard for me to bring myself to go back into the house long enough to call you. Now I know what I have to do."

"What's that?"

"I have to remove the weapon and ammunition, and put everything back together so there's no sign that anyone has been in the house. Then I do want your help. I'm frightened just to touch the stuff, never mind carry them around in my car. Will you help me figure out how to get rid of them?"

"Call me when you're ready to leave there. I'll wait right here by my phone. We'll work something out."

Melanie went back outside, finished a third cigarette, making sure to throw the butts far enough out into the street so as to not catch Alice's eye. She returned to the house, thinking that surely Ralph was not intending to harm Alice. Her father could be stupid about some things some of the time, that was all this was. She could almost convince herself. But the divorce put everything in a different perspective. That had already revealed things about her parents that she'd rather not know. Like this.

Quickly Melanie went up the stairs, then back up into the attic. Muttering an anxious prayer, she carefully brought the rifle down and laid it on the bedroom floor. "Please, please God, don't let anyone come here while I am doing this."

She went back two more times, once for each of the heavy metal boxes. She closed the hatch, returned the closet to its previous condition, then carried each box down to her car and placed it in the trunk. She went upstairs again, looked around for something to put the rifle in, and found an old laundry bag at the bottom of her closet. The rifle also fit in the trunk of her car. She went back into the house, grabbed a Coke from the refrigerator and dialed Angela to say she was leaving. Then she drove off, missing her father by only a few minutes.

\*\*\*

The shaking didn't start until she pulled her car into a parking space in front of Angela's office building. The enormity of what she had done now threatened to overwhelm her. Her legs wobbled and tears ran down her face. Angela saw her through the window and quickly came out to envelop her in a big hug and bring her inside. Melanie was flushed and trembling, her tearful face swollen. "Hey there, girl," Angela cooed to her like a mother comforting a toddler. "What can be this bad?" She let Melanie simmer for a few minutes, extended one tissue to her, and then another, as Melanie tried to control the sobs that racked her body. Finally, the tears stopped and with swollen eyes, she gazed at Angela.

"I thought I'd be on my way to school by now. When I saw you a couple of days ago, I was so happy. I thought things had finally come together and at last something good was happening for me. Now there's this." She hiccupped and then drew in a deep breath to calm herself. Angela waited for her to continue.

"I'm still shocked at finding that rifle. Just the thought of it being in the trunk of my car frightens me," Melanie began. "But did I tell you that Dad bought a family cemetery plot and when he told me about it, gave me papers to sign so I could be buried there when the time came? That made me feel creepy."

Angela was surprised and concerned. "Was this recent?" she asked.

"I guess I didn't tell you. Dad was all excited that he had a chance to get this beautiful cemetery plot that was big enough for our whole family. Best of all for him, it's in the same town and near the home he grew up in. It's peculiar, but Dad sometimes goes off the deep end about stuff that no one else would think about." She paused before continuing. "I thought his timing was strange, just before I was heading out of state for school. It opened up for me all the times I had to be hospitalized because of my illness and the urges I had to overcome to keep from hurting myself. I wondered if he thought I might not come back alive." She shuddered at the thought. "It just occurred to me—he even made a comment that it would at least be an opportunity for Mom to be with her family if she really wanted to. I wondered what he meant by that. Maybe now I know—but I hope I'm wrong."

She began to cry again. When she stopped, she went into the Ladies' Room to wash her face. After she finished, both women sat looking at each other in troubled silence. What to do? Angela had to admit that business about the family plot soon followed by finding the weapon would upset anyone.

"Well," Angela broke the continuing silence, "That's a pretty heavy load. I don't recall ever having had so much to try to sort through in any counseling session I've ever had with anyone. Let's just let it all set for the moment. I am worn out. You must be too. I have a spare room. I think you should stay with me tonight. We'll be better in the morning when we've both had a good night's rest. You can feel safe at my house, so you'll be able to sleep well. That'll do you a lot of good. I don't have any immediate answers and I doubt that if I did, they'd be worth anything."

***

They soon left Angela's office and drove the short distance to her home. Melanie wrapped herself in one of Angela's colorful flannel robes, then sat down in front of the TV and watched a comedy show as Angela made them bowls of chicken soup for supper. By ten o'clock, both felt tired enough to want to turn in and get some sleep. During the night, Angela was awakened once by Melanie's voice shouting, "No!" followed by sounds of her thrashing. Angela lay awake for a while after that listening for anything else. After a time, hearing nothing more, she fell into a fitful doze that lasted until morning.

The next day was a Wednesday, normally a light day for Angela. She called her office early that morning and asked her secretary to try to reschedule her appointments to the following day, or at least to later that afternoon. She moved around quietly as she showered and dressed, so as to not wake Melanie.

The teapot was singing away on the stove when Melanie came down to the kitchen. The house was filled with the smell of bread toasting, reminding her that her stomach was still pretty empty from the day before. She smiled briefly at Angela, then sat down at the kitchen table, and put her head in her hands.

"Are you all right?"

"I know I had a nightmare but I can't remember it."

"I think I have an idea about the rifle, but let's have some breakfast first. Then we can talk and see if it makes any sense."

Angela's friend Bud was a town police officer. He was usually the best source of advice when Angela had questions that could involve law enforcement. She sometimes asked Bud to help her out when she reached an impasse with a troubled youngster. He was good at being helpful without being heavy about it. If Melanie agreed, Angela would call Bud and see if she could meet him for coffee later that morning to ask for advice about how to help one of her clients. She wouldn't have to give away Melanie's name. They talked about it for a few minutes, then Melanie shrugged and agreed. "I don't have many options, it seems. And I trust what you have told me about Bud."

Angela made the call. She spoke into the phone for a few moments, and then peered around the corner of the doorway to ask, "Bud wants me to bring the rifle so he can look at it. Is it okay with you if I take it along when I go to meet him?"

"Sure, as long as you don't feel funny about doing that. But why does he want to see it?"

"He said something about checking the serial number."

After Angela finished talking with Bud, both women went outside to pack the weapon into the trunk of her car. Then Angela drove off to the coffee shop. After about an hour, when she returned from her consultation, she told Melanie that Bud couldn't do much to help her. He said the rifle hadn't been reported missing and they had no other information on it. Bud had given Angela a run-down on the weapon, which she repeated for Melanie.

She began, "It's an M-1, probably Korean War or earlier vintage, nothing unusual. It's former Army stock, but has no clip. It's been very well maintained. These models now tend to be mainly used for target practice. The breech is empty. The weapon isn't loaded."

Hearing that, Melanie felt the blood drain from her face as she realized that neither she nor Angela had thought about that possibility. Noticing her pallor, Angela paused and waited. Melanie's thoughts raced. Ralph would not be negligent about leaving a loaded weapon lying around. If the weapon were loaded when she found it in the attic, it could have signaled her father's intent to shoot her mother. And if it had been loaded, what if she had accidentally discharged it when she picked it up or when she brought it downstairs? She gripped the arms of her chair. Angela asked Melanie, "What's the matter?"

Melanie told her the thoughts that had just occurred to her. Angela responded, "But none of that happened. This is enough to try to sort out." Then Angela continued her recitation. "Bud thought the rifle hadn't been fired in quite a while. If you want him to, Bud could impound it, but he'd have to search out and notify the rightful owner, and then question him about it. I declined that offer, at least for the moment." When Angela paused, Melanie said how angry her father would be if that happened.

"Then," Angela continued," if there is nothing illegal about him owning and possessing a weapon, the rifle would have to be returned to Ralph."

What would Ralph do if he had the gun in his hands once again? Melanie was obviously concerned about that or she would not have taken the rifle in the first place. "That's not what I want," Melanie responded. "He can't have it back unless my mother is absolutely safe, and I am too. Maybe not giving it back to him is what it takes for us to be sure about that."

Angela asked, "How about telling your mother and getting her advice?" When Melanie hesitated to answer her, Angela insisted, "Someone beside you needs to know what the situation is. Let's try to do that today. I think you need to be away from here as soon as you can and get on with your plans to start school. The divorce is not your issue. That's between Alice and Ralph, and that's where the question of how to handle the disposal of this weapon belongs. Maybe Ralph would agree to get rid of it if he knew how its just being there has already affected us. If Alice agrees to approach him on that basis, do you think it would be worth a try?"

Melanie remained silent.

"You know, Melanie, sometimes you have to play hardball. I think your mother would be willing to do that for you."

Melanie didn't know what to do or how to begin. She sat quietly, turning Angela's suggestion over in her mind, trying to imagine what her mother would do, and then her father. She saw it all as a calculated risk. Angela left her alone, sitting in the kitchen with a fresh cup of tea. Some time later, she heard Melanie's chair being pushed back from the table. The sound of running water indicated that she was finished, and was now rinsing her dishes.

Angela returned to the kitchen to ask her, "Made up your mind?"

"I think so. The divorce is between them. I'm a casualty of that war, so to speak. Let's get Mom in on this so I can get away from here fast."

# Alice

Alice placed an early morning call to Phoebe to inform her that the weapon was now missing. Ralph had lied to Hubert about the rifle and ammunition being at Penelope's. He moved them—he said—to another hiding place in the house. Now he claimed they were gone. Ralph insisted he no longer had the weapon and ammunition, and he didn't know where they were. Alice was just plain tired of all his deceptions. Moreover, she was afraid of what this latest episode might mean. Now more than ever, Alice wanted the divorce over with. The business still remaining between her and Ralph was highly contentious—mainly it consisted of how to segregate their financial assets. Now the question of the missing weapon represented not just an additional burden, but a possible threat.

Phoebe talked with Hubert. It was a very energetic conversation. Hanging up the phone, Phoebe thought Hubert acted like he was trying to conceal something from her. She wondered what was going on.

Actually, Hubert had just advised Ralph that it would be a good time to level with Phoebe about the cemetery plot. Let her tell Alice. It would be a tough revelation to have to make, but now it seemed that everyone but Alice and Phoebe knew about it. It was only a matter of time before someone else brought it up. If that information didn't come from Ralph, it could look to Alice like he was planning to do away with her. Hubert spent a lot of time arguing about this with Ralph. He still hadn't convinced him to concede by the time of Phoebe's call.

Now there was this new information about the missing weapon, and Ralph was caught in a lie as to its whereabouts. Hubert castigated his client about not leveling with him, and all but threatened to sever his relationship with Ralph. He forcefully insisted that Ralph move out of the house—at least until things settled down, assuming that they ever did. Later that day, after some more heated discussion, Ralph finally conceded to Hubert's demands.

Distracted by the news of the missing rifle, and by his confrontation with Ralph, Hubert still hadn't quite decided how to broach the topic of the cemetery plot. Now he decided to just tell it to Phoebe straight out and let her tell Alice. He didn't relish doing it, but he called Phoebe to break that news.

After Hubert's revelation, Phoebe became very nervous. She didn't know what to make of it all, so she spoke informally to the judge; they had a lengthy conversation before the judge made a suggestion. His advice was to wait until they knew what the missing weapon really signified. The judge then invited Hubert to come see him.

Weapons were one thing, the judge thought, but even he had been surprised by the unusual story of the cemetery plot. He wanted to hear what Hubert had to say about it. He couldn't quite figure out whether that meant there was a real threat to Alice. Until the weapon showed up, there was no way for anyone to tell for sure. Ralph had not broken any law, but the judge didn't want to wait for that to take action, possibly in the form of a restraining order, if it looked like that might be necessary. Until there was reason to believe something had to be done, the judge preferred to wait. The result was that the judge slowed things down by refusing to set another court date until he had some satisfactory answers to the more immediate questions.

\*\*\*

Alice decided to call Eric that evening and ask his opinion about the whole mess. She was thoroughly mystified, and acutely worried. She needed to talk this over with someone who was not immersed in the situation. Eric went over and over the particulars, questioning Alice thoroughly, preventing her from lunging down purely speculative paths.

"Just the facts, ma'am, as my neighbor Joe Friday would say," Eric insisted. "I have always found that to be great advice when faced with things that have so much ambiguity attached to them. Usually they turn out not to be so mysterious after all."

As their conversation finally began to wind down, Eric abruptly said, "Tell you what, Alice. I have been planning to come east again at the end of the month to firm up a deal. I could just as easily be there the first of the week. I am already well-prepared for the business meetings, and concerned enough about you, that I will have my secretary make the arrangements right now."

Alice was relieved, and thankful for his generosity toward her.

"I'm giving you an assignment. We've covered the facts pretty well. Now I'm going to ask you to think outside the box. What are some other options if Ralph really doesn't have the rifle? And, you actually need to spend some energy to visit the "scene of the crime" to look for other clues. Take your time. Think things through. You're a clever woman. I'm sure that by the time I see you, you'll have a couple of alternative explanations for whatever this turns out to be."

*** 

Next morning Alice left the house to go to work at the usual time. A couple of hours later, she was back at home. She parked in the street, her car completely visible. If Ralph showed up, this would warn him of her presence. She went down to the basement, got a 6-foot ladder and carried it up to the second floor. She took a short break to catch her breath, and thought about what few things they usually stored up there. A few minutes later, ladder in position, she ascended. Boxes of Christmas ornaments greeted her. A bit farther from the opening lay a couple of smaller boxes that contained children's books. She saw a copy of *Winnie-the-Pooh* poking out the top of one box. There were a couple of well-worn Dr. Seuss books in the box as well. Alice recalled how much Melanie loved the Pooh stories, and how much she loved Teddy bears in general. She stood quietly for a few minutes to take a closer look at the space. The area used for storage was floored with plywood, but the greater part of this attic was unfinished. Had the rifle somehow slipped beneath the plywood flooring? Was there enough space between the flooring, insulation and the bedroom ceiling beneath, to accommodate it? Could it possibly still be there? Where had Ralph placed the stuff when he put it up here? There was nothing that pointed to answers to any of her questions.

Studying the boxes of books once again, Alice recalled Melanie's extensive family of Teddy bears. It had grown over the years. She recollected the day when Stan arrived with the rental truck filled with Melanie's belongings. She remembered how the stuffed animals and the bags of clothing and other goods lay scattered across the cargo bed. Everything was revealed lying in jumbled piles when Stan and Ralph opened the back of the truck. A tear rolled down her cheek as she remembered Stan's and Melanie's stricken faces and their emotional parting in the street in front of the house.

Ralph helped his daughter carry her things up to her bedroom that day. There Melanie carefully sorted them, separating that which could be stored from those she immediately needed. The boxes of children's books went up into this attic at that time. The Teddy bear collection originally lived on Melanie's bed, but in the past few months Alice did not recollect having seen them. Idly, she wondered what became of the bears. Alice thought she recalled Melanie carefully placing them in plastic bags and putting them away somewhere. They were not to be seen in the attic.

"Well," she sighed as she returned to the task at hand, "now I've seen it and I don't feel as though I have had any insights from it." She let herself down, carried the ladder back to the basement and prepared to leave the house.

***

The phone rang as Alice was reaching for her keys. It was Angela. "Have you got a few minutes to talk to us?"

"Sure. Who's 'us'? Do you mean you and Melanie?"

"Yes, Melanie spent last night here. Perhaps you thought she was on her way to school. She arrived here very upset. She needs to talk with you. I'll put her on."

Melanie's voice wavered, "Hello? Mom?"

"Hi, Honey," Alice's voice was brisk. "What's the matter?"

"Mom?" Then, after a lengthy hesitation, Melanie began to cry. "It was me. I did it."

"What do you mean, Sweetheart?"

"I took the rifle and the boxes of ammunition, and now I don't know what to do with them."

Alice was shocked, but at the same time relieved. Angela's voice came back on the other end of the phone. "She's very upset. She doesn't want you to say anything to anyone until we've talked about and resolved the issue of disposal. Melanie needs to be certain that the stuff is secured and away from her father."

"When will that be decided?" Alice was concerned about Melanie having taken the weapon and how that might now affect her.

"What do you think about my asking a policeman friend who sometimes helps with difficult clients and situations? Bud has already seen the rifle. He immediately checked to see if it had been loaded. It wasn't, but neither Melanie nor I had thought about that possibility. He said it hadn't been fired in a long time. He offered to impound it. If he did, he'd have to try to locate and notify the owner, then ask him to come in to answer some questions to claim his weapon. Under normal circumstances that would take some time, but in this case we know who the owner is."

"Angela, both attorneys know the rifle and ammunition are

missing. We'd have to tell them if the stuff turned up, and if it was impounded, who had it and where it was being kept. Ralph would find out pretty quickly, and from more than one source. So as soon as we tell anyone, we have to assume that everyone knows."

Melanie came back on the phone. "Mom, I think this is getting pretty complicated. Maybe you had better come to Angela's to help us figure out what to do about it."

# Melanie

They sat around Angela's kitchen table drinking tea. The discussion had circled around several times. Melanie still had the rifle and ammunition in the trunk of her car. She was scared about having taken them. She only did that to protect her mother. How could she just leave them in the house once she had found them in the attic? Melanie was afraid that if Ralph got his rifle back, he'd use it to threaten Alice. When Melanie said she'd never intended for this to turn into such a big hairy deal involving so many people, Angela made a joke about there being safety in numbers.

At first, Alice wasn't sure what to say except that the stuff could not be brought back into the house. She couldn't handle that. She couldn't trust what Ralph might do. Then Melanie mentioned the cemetery plot.

Alice was taken by surprise. "What do you mean? What cemetery plot?"

The papers Ralph sent Melanie were in her car. She got them, brought them into the house and spread them out across the kitchen table. There was a schematic of the plot, and a couple of grainy photos. Alice was astonished. "What's this all about?"

"Dad bought this plot for the family in a cemetery near

where he grew up. It's big enough for all of us. He sent everyone the forms to sign so they can be buried there. He sent everyone a diagram of the plot and how he planned where we'd all be placed."

Alice studied the drawing, a slight frown creasing her face. There was a place for Melanie and a place for a husband if she should marry. Another place was reserved for Penelope. There was one designated for Ralph, one marked "Bunny", and one for Alice.

"This is curious. Does your father have a pet rabbit?" A smile tugged at the corner of her mouth.

Three sets of eyes peered at the place Alice now indicated. "See this? Who—or what—is Bunny?" Alice had a pretty good idea as to what the name might mean. "Looks like Ralph's got a girl friend."

"Mom," said Melanie, "he was all excited about how the plot has a lovely view of a small pond. Maybe he goes there to have picnics and there's a rabbit that shows up that's tame and begs for food."

"Maybe it isn't so innocent, and the creature is one who comes dressed in a Playboy bunny outfit."

Angela interrupted them. "I hate to be the heavy and bring all this good fun to an end, but we still have work to do. We have a serious decision to make. We need to do that at once if we're actually going to accomplish anything today."

They quickly agreed that the best solution would be to ask Bud to impound the stuff. That way when they told the lawyers about it, they could say it was being safely held in legal custody until Ralph could claim it.

When Bud finally arrived at Angela's, he was prepared to leave with the goods. He brought along a storage box and custody form which he filled out as he carefully looked everything over. He handed Melanie a receipt for all of it—a 30-06 caliber M-1 rifle and two boxes of 500 rounds each of 22-caliber ammunition. Once Bud was gone, the innocuous-looking receipt that lay on the kitchen table was the only connection Melanie now had with the stuff that so badly haunted her from the moment she first saw it barely 24 hours earlier. None of them wanted to give Ralph back the gun and ammunition. Now that decision would reside with someone who had the right kind of authority to make it.

Alice called Phoebe to tell her what had taken place. Phoebe felt that they chose the right course of action regarding the weapon. She was relieved that things now seemed to be under control. She had just gotten off the phone with Hubert and was glad that Alice had already learned about the cemetery plot. She was still a bit steamed about Hubert's blunt disclosure of it to her; she didn't want her anger to color the information about the rifle and ammunition that she now would have to share with him. Phoebe wanted to thoroughly review all the details with Hubert, and give him a chance to bring Ralph up to date. Then she wanted to set up an informal meeting for everyone with the judge in order to clear the air. She asked if Melanie and Angela would be willing and able to attend if she could accomplish this within the next couple of days. Angela was willing, Melanie reluctant. School and her new beginning now beckoned more urgently than ever.

***

Alice finished her discussion with Phoebe without mentioning Bunny. Things were already a little too complicated. Turning now to Angela and Melanie, she said that Phoebe was pretty certain Hubert wouldn't try to fight to get Ralph's gun and ammunition returned to him, at least not yet. That could happen later, but Hubert would more likely want to wait and see what would happen in the informal meeting in the judge's office. Phoebe said it was important for Melanie to speak with the judge about her illness.

"It'll help the judge to understand what you've been up against, and how you have been able to overcome it enough to now be starting a new life for yourself," Angela encouraged Melanie. "He'll ask you why you took the weapon and ammunition from the house to begin with. You'll need to spend some time thinking about how you want to answer that question."

"Phoebe will try to get the meeting organized so as to free you to leave for school as quickly as possible," Alice said. "I expect the judge is trying to sort out a lot of things he's heard from both sides. This new business about there being a weapon and now a cemetery plot has just added more to his list of things to be concerned about when he reviews the divorce petition. This meeting is supposed to clear the air, and I hope it does that quickly. If there are tough questions, you can bet those will be aimed at your father and me, not at you."

Melanie finally agreed.

# Alice

When Alice got home, a message from Eric was waiting on her voicemail. He had just arrived in Boston and wanted to know if she still wanted to have dinner with him? He'd meet her wherever she'd like. She was to call him at his hotel. Alice looked forward to this. Now she had something to tell him, and it was good news for a change. They met in Quincy at a waterfront restaurant both could easily get to. They greeted each other warmly and were soon so engaged in talking, the waiter had a hard time interrupting the flow of conversation long enough to take their orders.

She told him about visiting the "scene of the crime" as he had challenged her to do, and described the attic to him. He thought for a moment and then asked, "And where were the Teddy bears? Have they turned up yet?"

Alice had a sudden flash—Melanie must have been looking for them to take them with her to school when she came across the rifle. Why hadn't that occurred to her?

Eric laughed when she told him her instant thought. "It's elementary, my dear. What did I tell you? Things just aren't that hard to figure out." He laughed even harder when she reacted by swatting the air near his cheek.

"Alice, you haven't changed a bit." He gave her a teasing,

168

smug look. "You always hated it whenever I was right. You still do." His expression became serious. "Your daughter is very brave to have taken on so much responsibility, and to have done that to prevent anything bad from happening to her mother. You're a very lucky woman. Everything will turn out just fine for you."

They enjoyed the meal and talked for quite a while afterward. Eric would always be on her side. If things got rough, she could always pick up the phone and call him. Wherever they were, they could at least talk. He told her about now gaining a partner for the east coast expansion. They had decided to open the new gallery on Lexington Avenue in New York City. It had been a tough choice between Boston and New York. New York would be operationally more expensive, but they believed it would be their best chance to expand the business quickly and successfully.

Alice was happy for him, wishing him luck. "You know where you are headed right now, but I still have to revive my job search. Working full time and then coping with everything that has happened with this divorce have really set back the effort I need to make to start all over. I'm getting too old for this stuff."

"We're the same age, Alice. If I can start up another gallery, you can succeed at what you have to do. Over and over again, you've shown me that you can do anything you put your mind to. Speaking of that, take me seriously about what I'm going to say to you. When I came back the last time, I wanted to ask your help to invite the friends from our college days to serve as a nucleus of advisors that we could go to and use as a sounding board for a gallery in Boston, and who could direct us to potential sponsors for the project. After you told me about divorcing Ralph, I let go of that idea, and decided I'd just keep in touch and see what happened with you. The last time you called, I became much more anxious about your situation. That gave me two good reasons to come back here—one was your safety and my concern for you; the other was that I'd love to have you involved with this gallery. You're looking for a new job. I didn't feel comfortable saying this earlier, because it might have sounded like I was trying to solve your problems for you. But now I think it's timely. The gallery is going to be in New York, not Boston, but it's going to be very exciting if we succeed. We have a solid business plan. We've done this before, and we see every reason to believe we'll do well with the new venture. I know how hard you work, and how much you could contribute to this project. Think about that, and we'll talk about it again once your divorce gets resolved."

Alice scarcely knew how to respond. "You're certainly full of surprises, Eric. Yes, I will think about it, a lot." She hugged him, thanked him for his solicitude and promised that as soon as she had recovered from the shock of his offer to her, she'd let him know.

***

That night Alice fell into a deep sleep. As the moon rode serenely through the heavens, shining its cool light through her bedroom window, Alice encountered a figure emerging from the depths of her subconscious mind. The figure came into view, then into focus. It was the mystery woman from the fish auction. Alice stood facing her in this dream. Neither spoke. As Alice slightly turned her body, so did the woman. As she raised her arm, so did the woman. Alice reached toward the woman, and she reached toward Alice. Their fingertips met, but without sensation of touch. Fingers and hands came together and then retreated. They stood, smiling and staring at each other. Alice again saw her strange costume, her rumpled face, her spare smile. Again she experienced the intensity of the woman's strength, her courage, her authenticity. A few moments passed, both figures standing quite still, facing each other. Then Alice stepped back; the woman did the same; she receded, and was gone. Alice's face twitched in her sleep to form a transitory smile. She turned over in the bed, pulled the sheets up around her shoulders and drifted off into tranquil slumber.

***

170

The next afternoon, Phoebe called Alice to let her know the meeting with the judge was now set for 7:45 on the following morning. Phoebe said that the judge had been in a "take no prisoners" mood, and had emphasized that if everyone showed up on time, he could squeeze them in before his first court session was scheduled to begin. He had imparted the same message to Hubert, telling him that he was willing to try to have this meeting so that when the actual divorce proceeding was scheduled, that would move quickly.

Everyone assembled on time, separating into groups as if in a church for a wedding. Melanie and Angela sat on the left side of the courtroom behind Phoebe and Alice. Hubert and Ralph sat on the right side. A middle-aged woman quietly entered and sat at the rear near the closed door. Alice turned at the sound of the door opening and closing, curious if someone else had been expected. She saw an unfamiliar woman, and wondered who she might be. At the sound, the judge, who was sitting at his desk at the bench, looked up from the pages he had been reviewing and asked, "Ma'am, are you here for this meeting?"

The woman looked flustered. "No, Judge. My attorney asked me to meet him in here before 8 a.m. He told me the room would be empty at this hour, and we could speak privately for a few minutes."

"As you can see, the room is in use right now, and this too is a private matter. Perhaps you'd step outside into the vestibule and meet your attorney there."

"Yes, Judge." Bunny picked up her things and made a quick exit.

"Okay," the judge began. "I'm ready. Let's get this over with. I've decided that the best way to avoid interruptions is for me to ask each of you separately to come into my office. I'll begin with the young lady, the daughter."

Looking at Angela, he asked, "Who are you? Are you with the daughter?"

Angela responded, "I am, Judge." Then she gave him her name and professional reason for being in the room.

"Come along, then. Both of you follow me." He walked

back from the bench, opened a door in the paneling that was nearly invisible to anyone seated in the courtroom, and closed it after them.

"Young lady, I understand that you are trying to get on the road to go to school, and it has taken a lot of your time and effort to have achieved this new beginning."

"Yes sir," Melanie said softly. "But I just couldn't leave if something was going to happen to my mother." Then she told the judge her whole story. When she had finished, the judge turned his attention to Angela.

"You came to support your client. How do you think she's doing?"

"She's doing just fine, Judge. She's been through a lot in the last few days."

He turned to Melanie. "I've seen some young adults that have had problems, even some like what you've told me about. You've worked hard to get yourself back on track. Your parents should be proud of you. They are both adults. They can settle their own differences. You are free to leave now. Good luck to you, young lady."

They thanked the judge and followed him back into the courtroom.

Angela leaned over and whispered to Phoebe, "We'll wait outside." She handed Phoebe the impoundment receipt. "You may need this."

The judge then addressed Phoebe. "Ladies first." Alice and Phoebe rose from their seats and followed him through the door.

"We don't have a lot of time to spend on this, so let me come right to the point," the judge began.

Turning to Alice, he asked, "Do you think your husband intends to harm you? Or, do you think it's all just a matter of unfortunate circumstances and bad timing?"

"I wouldn't have thought he meant to harm me, but now I can't say that for sure. I guess if I had thought about that at all over the months when I saw that rifle and ammunition on at least a weekly basis, I would have done something to get rid of them. But that stuff has been in the house for years. I guess I've been so used to them being around that I've never thought of them as a threat to me."

"Well, your daughter wasn't trusting of what she thought his motives might be. She took action. That was commendable of her. She said the stuff had been impounded by a police officer and there's a receipt for it. Do you have it?"

Phoebe handed it to him. The judge looked at it intently, and then chuckled. Looking up from it, he asked, "Did either of you read this?"

Phoebe replied, "It was just handed to me before we came in here with you. Why, what is it?"

"The ammunition doesn't fit this weapon. They are of two separate calibers. Does he have another weapon?"

Alice thought for a few moments. "Some years ago, Ralph had a 22-calibre pistol."

"Does he still have it?"

"I think he sold it to one of his friends. I haven't seen it in a long time."

"Why do you think he holds on to the ammunition if he doesn't still have the weapon to use it?"

"I don't know what to think," Alice replied.

"I can only act on what we know for sure," the judge said. "If you are both comfortable with me doing this, I'll insist it all remains impounded until after the divorce has been decreed. I assume you're getting close to that. He hasn't done anything illegal and he does have a right to have his stuff returned to him. I don't think he has a police record. He could go out right now — not too far from this courthouse, and buy any weapon he wanted, with the right caliber ammunition for it. I would hope that is not what he intends to do. Then there's this cemetery plot. Do you know what that's all about?"

Alice admitted she was shocked when Melanie told her about it and showed her the plot plan. "It's the kind of thing Ralph might do on the spur of the moment. I can't explain it. He can be impulsive about things. Another surprise for me was a name I'd not seen before. It was certainly not a family member. That makes me believe he has a girlfriend. He has concealed that from me pretty well."

The judge smiled. "I wondered why that woman came into the courtroom so early this morning. It was probably her. I've seen that happen before. They can't seem to stay away."

Alice made a small choking noise. Phoebe beamed at the judge. "Thank you, Your Honor."

"If we're finished here, it's time for me to talk to the boys."

When the judge appeared again in the courtroom, the clerk was already there setting the microphones and distributing paperwork for the first session of the day. "Just a few more minutes," the judge said as he walked past the man.

He gestured to Ralph and Hubert. They followed him into his private office. Inside the inner office, the door closed, the judge now began to listen to Ralph's explanation about the weapon, the ammunition and the cemetery plot. The judge asked him where he had gotten the rifle, how long he had owned it, what he used it for, what caliber it was. He asked the same questions about the ammunition. When Ralph finished his recital, he added, "I never stopped to think about this aspect of it, but the shells are a different caliber than the rifle so they could never be used together."

Hubert quickly said, "You mean you couldn't have used any of that to take a shot at your wife?"

"No," Ralph replied, "I could not have."

"Do you own another weapon?" the judge asked.

"Not any more." Ralph replied. "I had a pistol, but sold it a few years ago."

"Do you have a receipt for that transaction?" the judge questioned, giving both men a stern look.

"I may have, but if I do, I have no idea where it is," Ralph said.

The judge then asked if they were aware that Melanie took the weapon and that both rifle and ammunition were now impounded. They acknowledged that Phoebe had told Hubert, and Hubert dutifully passed that information along to Ralph.

"Judge," Hubert began, "my client has done nothing illegal."

"Are you saying that you think the weapon should be returned to him right now?" The judge's tone sounded incredulous.

Hubert stammered, "Let's just say I was making a point about my client."

The judge followed up, "Let's say you have just made your point. Let's also say that if I hear your client has another weapon, or uses a weapon to threaten anyone, I'll throw the book at him. Do you both understand me?"

They did. The judge then excused them so he could robe for the session now being announced outside in the courtroom.

***

Bunny stood in a far corner of the vestibule near a group of people milling about, as if she were waiting for someone. She could move in closer and blend in, if any of the women she was observing turned to look in her direction. She saw Ralph and Hubert emerge from the courtroom. Ralph glanced toward her and then quickly turned away. She saw him scowl, and wondered what had happened inside. She would make it her business to find out soon.

All at once, Melanie broke away from her group of women as they stood in a tight knot, talking. She headed for the exit. At that moment, Ralph called to her, waving his hands. "Wait! Wait a minute! Melanie!" He hurried to intercept her. "Melanie, it's all right. I didn't want you to leave for school without me telling you that. You've been very brave in every way. Honey, I love you and I don't want you to worry about any of this. I'm sorry you were frightened. I'm not a man who would hurt anyone. I promise you that, no matter what. Please believe me."

Melanie looked at her father and said, "Okay, Dad. We'll see if you're telling the truth now." She gave him a quick smile as she turned toward the exit.

Ralph then approached Alice as Angela was saying her good-byes. He heard Angela's voice saying "…and call me any time if I can help." Alice and Angela hugged.

Bunny's heart sank as she watched Ralph come close to Alice. She saw the neediness in his face as he leaned toward her.

"Did you come to tell us what the judge said to you?" Phoebe asked.

"I came to apologize to Alice and to let you know that Hubert and I will work to get a settlement offer for you."

"Thanks for the good news," Phoebe responded.

Ralph moved closer to Alice as if to embrace her. "Who's Bunny?" Alice whispered in his ear.

Startled, he backed off. Bunny was relieved to witness that.

Until he spotted Ralph, Hubert had again been in earnest discussion with the security guard. Now he approached the group. "Time to talk," Ralph told him, taking his arm and steering him away. "Damn," said Ralph through clenched teeth. "Alice knows about Bunny."

Once Ralph and Hubert were outside the building, Bunny left the vestibule. Phoebe and Alice remained engaged in conversation. Alice was saying, "I'm relieved at the way the judge handled all of this. I'm also relieved that even if Ralph had a moment when he might have entertained the notion of getting rid of me, he couldn't have done it. I just can't imagine he'd ever do such a thing. But I never thought he'd lie to me either; so much for trusting one's spouse."

"You can't begin to imagine how many women have thought that, to their peril," Phoebe responded. "You don't know how fortunate you really are. Now that this is over, we need to get back to work on wrapping up the negotiations and making you a free woman once and for all. I doubt that now it'll be so difficult to deal with the boys. I think the whining stage is behind us. I'll be in touch." Phoebe left Alice feeling very hopeful about the situation.

***

That evening Alice had a meeting scheduled with Carrie. There were so many things she needed to talk about—the episode involving the missing weapon; Eric's help, and his appearance in Boston that he admitted he orchestrated just for her benefit, and just when she most needed his support; the myste-rious woman she had seen at the fish auction who had since appeared in a dream. She felt that was somehow significant. Then there was the night she spent in Bruce's arms.

Alice felt upbeat and energetic as she entered Carrie's of-fice. Carrie listened to everything Alice had to say, comment-ing every so often or asking a quick question about some detail. Carrie voiced particular concern about her brief affair with Bruce. She reminded Alice of the story about Ros. Alice told Carrie how stunned she had been that she had given in to him so easily. But when she thought about all she had gone through and was still trying to cope with, she thought that opportunity for Bruce to make his move on her was simply the straw that broke the camel's back. She described the conversation that she thought had ended that relationship. Carrie just smiled and suggested Bruce would continue to wait for her, at least for a while, but that wouldn't keep him from having affairs with other women.

When Carrie asked Alice how she now felt about Bruce, she described how the mysterious woman at the fish auction seemed to know everything that churned through Alice's mind, especially how disappointed she felt about herself after giving in to Bruce. But in the woman's gaze she experienced a peace-ful dispensation that inexplicably healed her anxieties. That helped her put her affair with Bruce into perspective as an im-portant milestone in learning to accept her own human frailties.

Alice had come a long way from the tentative, hesitant per-son she'd been when she first met Carrie. Alice had fledged and was ready to fly using her own wings. Carrie's last ques-tion to her was, "Did you figure out who the mystery woman of your dream might be?" When Alice responded with a hesitant," No, not yet," Carrie asked, "Doesn't she remind you of any-one?" Alice looked at her in amazement as a glimmer of rec-ognition tugged at the corners of her mind. Then Carrie burst out into full, rich laughter.

# Ralph

Hubert and I left the courthouse together, walked to the parking lot, and then went our separate ways. I sensed that Bunny was following me, but I didn't especially want to talk with her just then. What had she been thinking, to show up in the courtroom like that? It was lucky that no one identified her as my girlfriend. She's never before done anything that stupid. She picked a bad time to start. She has no claim on me to do something like that.

I drove off in a foul mood. I needed to be by myself so I could think about things. I never imagined Alice filing for divorce, but over the years of our marriage there had probably been more than a fair share of things I hadn't imagined could happen, but they did. Automatically I drove to the marina, parked the car, got out and headed toward the dock.

The broker stepped out of her office and intercepted me. "The surveyor was here yesterday. He spent about four hours on board. When he finished, I asked him if he found anything significant. He said there were just a couple of minor things that the buyer would probably not bother with for the sake of completing the transaction, and that he'd send a copy of his report to us by the end of the week. So that means we can complete the sale within the next ten days. Is your wife available to sign the papers with you, or should I try to arrange something different?"

I told her I'd ask Alice and let her know when I had an answer to that question. Then I thanked the broker for the news. I said, "I'm just going over there for a last look and to enjoy some of the better memories. Don't worry. I'll leave things just as they are."

I continued my long walk down the dock to my slip, and climbed aboard the boat. Immediately the thought struck me, "This is the last time I'll be on board this boat. There have been too many last times, and they've all come up too soon." I looked across the water to the house and saw a light go on. Alice must have just come home. I thought how once I might have called her and asked her to meet me for dinner at the marina. I could do that right now. She would probably turn me down, but if she agreed to have dinner with me, then maybe I could think of a way to talk her out of the divorce. Maybe I should try to do that. It would take some effort on my part and I'm way out of practice. Women usually come to me, not the other way around.

All these years our small family had been together as Melanie grew up, became a teenager and reached out for independence. Then suddenly we all seemed to go off in different directions. That began with Alice's first job, and then with her going back to school and the guy she met there and had that love affair with. There was Melanie's illness, and now here's Alice wanting a divorce. At this point, Melanie goes off to school probably never to return home again. If she did, where would that home even exist for her any more? As I thought about these things and hesitated, the light went off. Alice must be going out for the evening. Maybe she was celebrating the day's triumph with some of her friends. The one time in all these years I'd willingly call Alice to tell her where I was and that I didn't plan to show up at the house, she wouldn't be there to take the call. She had gone out. That's ironic; it was depressing to think how the tables had turned on me.

I decided to stay on the boat for the night. That would be

another "last" to add to my growing list. I'd call the house and leave Alice a voice message so she'd at least know where I was. Maybe I should think of a way to talk her out of the divorce. Today's events in the courthouse were really getting to me. Who would have thought things would happen this way? All the years this rifle has been in the house, and only now does it turn into such a big deal.

I spent some more time thinking about Melanie and all she had been through with her illness. I thought about all the pain that she and Stan had felt, especially during that first year. Today, the way that Melanie was ready to leave for school all by herself, without even saying good bye, really hurt. I thought I had experienced enough of grief and suffering from the divorce, but that was extra.

When I spotted Bunny at the court house, I wondered what she thought she was doing, showing up there. If she had offered to do that, I'm not sure I would have wanted her to, but it's too late for that now. Did she think she would find something out about me that she didn't already know and would make her not want to live with me? If so, I don't care. Bunny's good at figuring things out for herself. Whatever I seem to think about her anymore all comes down to the house I'm building for us. Well, that nails it.

# Bunny

I know Ralph wanted me to stay away from the courthouse, but I had to see what was going on. I didn't know what to think about the rifle, so if that was going to be the topic for discussion, I wanted to listen and learn anything I could. I guess I was reaching a little too far because the judge noticed me sitting in the back and asked me to leave the courtroom. I went outside into the entrance hall and decided to wait. I still wanted to find out any information that I could. Now I'd have to get it from the Source himself.

Outside in the vestibule, I stood around watching people scurry to their offices, or trying to find where to report for jury duty. Small groups started to gather and then move down the hallways as the court's business began for the day. They looked like they might be plaintiffs, witnesses, defendants, and their lawyers. They took up a lot of space hanging around outside of the various courtrooms, waiting for the call to come inside and have their turn before the bench. I didn't envy any of them.

For a while I wondered what it would be like to work in a place like this, and decided anyone who did must really want to be here. Then a larger group of mostly women came through the entrance. I sidled over to stand near enough to look like I was one of them. I needed some camouflage. I didn't want to be caught out in the open when Ralph and the others came out of their courtroom. I thought that might happen soon, as the crowd outside waiting for that judge had begun to grow.

I saw Ralph's daughter and her friend come out. They stood talking, obviously waiting for the others. Then Alice and her lawyer came out of the courtroom and joined them. They seemed to be having quite a conversation. Then the daughter broke away from them to leave, and there was Ralph, running across the vestibule and calling her name. They seemed to speak only a few short sentences before the daughter headed for the door. I know Ralph noticed me, but instead of coming over to me, he turned and walked toward Alice. When I saw him try to embrace her, I was sure I had come off second best. He looked intent about whatever it was he was saying to her. It looked like he might be trying to talk her into reconciling. That would be bad for me. I couldn't allow it to happen. He's building that house for me—or I should say, for us. If he did go back to Alice, where would I live? I am really going to have to concentrate on pinning him down once and for all. This whole thing seems to have gotten him confused about what he should be paying attention to. What does that lawyer of his think he's doing, anyway? Let's cut the nonsense and just get a settlement everyone can live with so this can all be over.

When Ralph and his lawyer left the courthouse, I followed them. I figured I could catch up with them and then I'd have a chance to talk with Ralph. With high heels on, I couldn't keep up with the two men, who were walking so fast they might as well have been running. Men seem to like women to wear these things on our feet. Then they take advantage of it by walking away, unless they want something from us. When they reached the parking lot, they took off in different directions. Ralph all but ran to his car, got in and drove off. He knew I was there trying to catch up with him. What kind of game was this? Now I was getting angry. Something was going on and I needed to know what it was.

\*\*\*

Finally I got to my car. I decided to drive by the house to see if his car was there, although I doubted it would be. I was right. Maybe he had gone to the boat. Sometimes he did that when he wanted a chance to think about things without being disturbed. There was his car, in the marina parking lot.

Now that I had found him, I was a little nervous about just walking down the dock and climbing on board the boat. I had a pair of walking shoes in the car and was glad I could take off the heels and put those on. For this job I would need all the comfort I could get. I thought for a few minutes whether I should just go to the boat and offer to be with him. It was either that or drive away and wait to see what would happen next. Ralph was a funny duck sometimes. He had to be upset by all this stuff, so I voted to take the chance and show up for him.

"What are you doing, tracking me down like this," was the reception I got.

"I care about you," was all I could think of to say to him. He turned his back to me.

"I thought you shouldn't be all alone after what you've been through lately." Am I in danger here? I was thinking that to myself, when he turned around to me, his face streaked with tears. This was a side of Ralph that I had never seen before.

"I guess I've screwed everything up," he sobbed.

"It'll all sort itself out. You'll see." I tried hard to act like I believed it. I didn't want him blaming me for this situation. I forbade myself to think about whether he had a gun with him.

I plunged ahead with the question I really didn't want to ask or hear him answer. "Ralph, do you think you want to get back together with Alice?"

"I don't know. I thought I might. But now I think my marriage is over for good. She wouldn't have me back." His shoulders were heaving.

"How do you know that? Did you ask her?" What was the matter with me? Had I somehow turned into the Good Samaritan?

"I just know it," he said. "And I don't want to talk about it."

That sounded like the Ralph I knew. I was so relieved.

I asked him if he wanted to freshen up and then go out to an early dinner. He said it sounded good to him. So we left the boat and walked back down the dock to use the rest rooms. We decided we'd drive to someplace where we could sit and talk without the chance we'd be interrupted by someone we knew. As he loosened up and began to relax a bit, I asked him, trying to make it sound as casual as I could, what had gone on in the judge's office that morning. He told me about the meeting he and Hubert had had with him. He was still incredulous at the judge even thinking he would now consider going out to buy a gun. That was the opening I was looking for to broach the subject of the rifle.

"What do you need that thing for if you haven't used it in years? Isn't it part of your past? What happens if it stays impounded? Don't the police just get rid of stuff like that?"

He seemed to take his time to think about how to answer me and finally didn't respond at all to what I had just asked. So I had to take the bull by the horns. I drew a deep breath. "Ralph, there's no delicate way to say this, but I have to. If I have any reason to think that I could be in danger by staying with you, then I have to say good-bye. I'm sorry, but you've been an entirely different person these past couple of weeks. Now I'm beginning to feel like I don't even know you."

"Does that mean you want to get rid of me now, after what I've just been through and after all that I've done for you?"

"No, it means that I want you back—the old "you". I want back the guy I fell I love with, that's all. If he isn't there, I'd have to go away. I'd cry a lot and hope I could get over him, but I can't stick with someone I don't know any more."

I had hoped I could move him beyond the emotional scene I had witnessed with his daughter and wife so that I could connect with him again. I knew I was now on shaky ground, and I was afraid of him like this, to boot. I didn't know what he might do next.

"Alice said something to me about why she was not willing to talk about trying to get our marriage back together. She said, "Where there's no trust, there can be no love.""

"Then you've learned something about relationships." I wanted to be sure he got that message.

When he said, "I hope so," I thought that maybe he had.

When we left the restaurant and went back to the marina, I thought a nice massage on the boat would help restore the Ralph I knew and wanted. After a while he told me that when the divorce was all over, we could take a trip, a sort of honeymoon.

# Alice

A day later, Alice met with Phoebe and together they finished putting the final touches on the settlement offer that reflected everything Alice wanted. If there had to be a "Plan B," it wouldn't be very different from this offer. Alice believed they had worked hard to be fair and that any change would mean a concession. She was not interested in anything like that.

As a precaution, and to resolve the issue of how much the house might be worth, Alice hired a licensed professional appraiser to report its current market value. This would carry a lot more weight than opinion, even one that might be somewhat well-informed. Alice asked for the house and a division of their remaining assets that left both her and Ralph with their individual retirement savings intact. Phoebe thought that made sense and was prepared to meet with Hubert to see if he and Ralph could agree.

When Phoebe extended the offer, Hubert told her that he had reason to believe that Ralph first wanted to talk with Alice about reconciling their differences. He thought it was late in the game for Ralph to be thinking about anything like that, and told Phoebe he really couldn't predict what Ralph might decide to do. Hubert wasn't taking any bets on how Ralph would react to Alice's offer, but he agreed to take it to his client. Phoebe sent a courier to deliver the settlement proposal to Hubert's office. Personally, Hubert hoped Ralph would concur with the offer. He had a new client that was now demanding more of his time, so he would be happy to be finished with Ralph. When he reviewed the proposal with Ralph, he stressed the fact as forcefully as he could, that there was no guarantee if Ralph refused this offer, there would be another as good.

***

Phoebe called Alice the next morning to tell her they had an agreement. She would ask the judge for a court date as soon as possible.

When Alice picked up her mail that afternoon, there was a thick envelope with a corporate return address. It was a job offer, and in fact, it was one she wanted. She had already decided she could not accept Eric's offer and told him that a couple of days after they met for dinner. He wasn't surprised. If she had accepted, it would have been inconsistent with the Alice he knew—she would not go from divorcing Ralph to working for Eric. Alice wanted a clean slate to start her life all over again, this time on her own terms.

Acceptance of this offer meant she would be relocated to Seattle. The salary offered was generous, a significant increase for her. She would be expected to start the new job in no more than a month's time. The company would move her. She was so excited she could barely contain herself. She called Melanie and Phoebe, and left messages for Eric, Carrie and Angela.

"You can accept the job but don't say or do anything until after we've gone before the judge," Phoebe cautioned an exuberant Alice. She would have to wait until she had the decree and a deed to the house in her own name before she could contact a realtor to find a buyer for her beloved home on the harbor. She would have to find a temporary place to live that was near her new company. Suddenly Alice had a lot to do. But first, she had to accept the job offer.

When she called Bruce, he wished her well and wondered if they would ever see each other again. Alice thanked him for his friendship and replied that she didn't know, but she would always think of him affectionately.

***

Once again, Alice, Ralph and their attorneys convened in the courtroom where they had gathered barely a week earlier. This time, after the initial formalities had been taken care of, the judge hammered his gavel on the desktop, and pronounced them divorced.

Alice and Ralph remained standing in silence as the judge left the courtroom. Then each turned to their lawyer. Phoebe was scooping up papers from her side of the table and placing them back in her briefcase. Looking up at Alice, she smiled and offered her congratulations. They left the courtroom together, pausing in the vestibule. Hubert and Ralph stood in conversation a few feet away.

Phoebe told Alice she had to meet another client in a few minutes, and asked if she'd like to walk back across the street with her. Alice automatically nodded, and turned to put on her jacket. Out of the corner of her eye she saw a woman emerge from the far corner of the vestibule and walk purposefully toward Ralph. Bunny saw Alice's glance and gave her a confident smile. She took Ralph's arm, turning him so that his back was to Alice.

She turned away and followed Phoebe out of the building. They stood for a few minutes, shaking hands and saying their good-byes. "You did yourself a real favor to take that job and move away," was Phoebe's parting comment. "With distance you'll get a better perspective on all of this. Good luck."

As Alice walked away from the court house, her unsettled feeling departed. It was still fairly early in the morning, and the day beckoned to her. She inhaled a lungful of fresh air, then walked to her car and drove home.

As she started up her front steps, she spied a great blue heron standing in the marsh at the edge of the water. The tide had turned and begun to rise. As each small wavelet washed ashore, the heron would scan the water to see if some morsel of food were being propelled in its direction. It could stand motionless for hours waiting for a small fish or an eel or a worm. Its patience seemed endless, but it was nearly always rewarded. The bird seemed both a blessing and a message. This place would always be a part of her. She stood for a few minutes watching as the bird struck the water and came up with a small fish which went straight down its gullet. The heron turned its head toward her, and then took flight with wide graceful wings. Alice walked up the steps and entered the empty house. She had a lot to do in the next couple of weeks. With the divorce now over, she felt its burden lifted from her shoulders. A few hours of manual labor would be good for her. She rolled up her sleeves and got to work.

In the middle of the day, Alice came back outside and sat on the step with her lunch. The tide had risen above the half-way mark, and now the heron was replaced by a small group of ducks, mostly mergansers and buffleheads, splashing and diving for the bait fish that were almost always present when the marsh grass was half covered by the rising water. She would miss these spontaneous performances.

Inside she had begun to pack her collection of decoys. Her aim had been to obtain one of each species she could observe in front of her house. She had just added a canvasback, the only duck that had been missing from the collection. "Just in time for them all to move to a new home," she thought sadly. As she sat there musing about the morning's events, the mailman came down the sidewalk and handed her the airplane tickets. He pointed toward the place next to the boat channel where he had caught a striper on the incoming tide the previous evening. As he turned to leave, he wished her good luck and happiness in her new life.

She opened the envelope to check her tickets and itinerary. She would leave in a few days and still had much to do to organize her departure. Her journey would take her from Boston to Seattle by way of Caspar, Wyoming. She would call Brad's mother later in the day to give her the flight information. Someone would meet her at the airport and take her to the ranch where the family would be awaiting her arrival. She sat there wondering what they thought about her coming, all these years after Brad's death. Mary was right that Alice needed to see his marker and help her scatter the rest of his ashes.

She and Mary would meet for the first time. They maintained a sporadic correspondence; after the year following Brad's death, it slowed to an annual Christmas letter. Alice never found the opportunity to visit the ranch. She still very much wanted to see where Brad grew up and learn more about that part of his life. His father passed away a few years ago; Mary continued living on the ranch with one of her married daughters and her family. The women planned that before sunrise, they would climb the hill where Brad's memorial stood, and release his remaining ashes into the dawn. Alice knew she would never forget Brad, but now it was time for closure.

*\*\**

In the middle of the afternoon, the phone rang. It was Bruce. "How did it go this morning at court? Is everything okay? Are you very busy? Want to have dinner with me tonight?"

"It was pretty much what we expected; the judge pounded the gavel on the bench so fast it nearly made my head spin. I guess he wanted my case to be off his desk as much as I did." Alice laughed. "I'm a free woman—finally. It'll take a while for me to get used to the thought." Alice hesitated. Bruce began to insist on taking her out for a celebration.

"Bruce, I have to get the house packed up and ready for the movers. I'm going to be gone soon. Once I'm all organized, maybe we can meet to say good-bye over a cup of coffee."

"Okay, Alice. Call me if you change your mind." She smiled as she hung up the phone.

# Acknowledgements

I am sincerely grateful to all my friends who read and commented on this novel. It is a far better story because of your generous support and encouragement. I'm especially thankful to N.D. for the conversations we shared about "espousing our brokenness"; those greatly influenced the development of the characters of Melanie, Alice, and the "mystery woman."

I extend my gratitude and admiration to Susannah Kaysen for her novel *Girl Interrupted* (1993), and Wally Lamb for *She's Come Undone* (1997). Each provided inspiration for Melanie. NOLO Press publishes *Divorce and Money*; it's a mine of information about what people fight about during divorce. It was a great reference for detailing Alice and Ralph's arguments about dividing up their assets.

For making my dream of publishing this book come true, I thank my agent and my publisher.

Printed in the United States
216668BV00003B/10/P

9 781606 936443